1

First published 2004 by Walker Books Ltd, 87 Vauxhall Walk, London SE11 5HJ

This volume contains abridged versions of *Sophie's Snail* (1988),
Sophie's Tom (1991), *Sophie Hits Six* (1991), *Sophie in the Saddle* (1993),
Sophie Is Seven (1994) and *Sophie's Lucky* (1995)

2 4 6 8 10 9 7 5 3 1

This book has been typeset in Minion Condensed

Printed in China

British Library Cataloguing in Publication Data:
a catalogue record for this book is available from the British Library

ISBN 0-7445-8375-6

www.walkerbooks.co.uk

Here Comes Sophie

WALKER BOOKS
AND SUBSIDIARIES
LONDON • BOSTON • SYDNEY • AUCKLAND

Here Comes Sophie

DICK KING-SMITH

illustrated by DAVID PARKINS

CONTENTS

CAST OF CHARACTERS

Tom

Tom is Sophie's cat. Sophie's parents didn't want a cat but Sophie did.

Beano

Beano is a large white rabbit with floppy ears and red eyes.

Puddle

Puddle is the family's dog. He is not always very well-behaved.

Sophie

Small and stocky, Sophie likes animals and wearing wellies and is determined to have a farm one day.

The Twins

Matthew and Mark are Sophie's older brothers, and almost always say the exact same thing at the exact same time.

Dad and Mum

Sophie's dad and mum have a big job looking after their three children, but a good sense of humour keeps them going.

Aunt Alice

Aunt Al is very old, very small, and lives in the Highlands of Scotland.

Dawn

Dawn and Sophie are not friends. Dawn once trod on one of Sophie's woodlice, and Sophie has never forgiven her.

Andrew

Andrew's father is a farmer, and Sophie likes to visit their farm.

Jo

Jo lives on a farm that Sophie visits on holiday. She's friendly and smells of pigs.

Lucky

Lucky is a pony that Sophie meets in Scotland. He belongs to the Grants, who live next door to Aunt Al.

INTRODUCTION

I took the character of Sophie from a girl whom I knew when I was young. She was small but very determined, she loved animals, and she told everyone that when she grew up she would marry either a farmer or a vet.

The words Sophie always uses when she's angry I borrowed from my son. He's fifty now, but when he was four or five and wanted to express his anger at someone, he would say, "You're mowldy, stupid and assive." Mowldy is wrongly spelt because he always pronounced the first syllable to rhyme with "owl".

Sophie's great-great-aunt is a carbon copy of my own Great-aunt Al, who died at the age of 94. Mind you, her father (my great-grandfather) lived to 102.

I'm so pleased about this book because I get such a lot of letters from children all over the world saying, "Please, please write another Sophie story," and I write back and say, "Sorry, I've done six and that's enough." But now *Here Comes Sophie*, and you can read all the best bits of the six stories. I hope you enjoy them.

"Wait for me," said Sophie. "I haven't got a snail yet."

ONE VERY SMALL FOOT

"What animal has got only one foot?" said the children's father. "I bet you can't tell me."

"I can!" said Matthew and Mark with one voice. As well as looking exactly alike, the twins nearly always said exactly the same thing at exactly the same time. Matthew was ten minutes older than Mark, but after that there had never been the slightest difference between them.

"Go on then," said their father. "Tell me. What animal's got only one foot?"

"A chicken standing on one leg!" they said.

"That's silly," said Sophie seriously.

Sophie was four, a couple of years younger than her brothers.

"That's silly," she said. "It would still have a foot on the other leg. Anyway, Daddy, there isn't really an animal that's only got one foot, is there?"

"Yes, there is, Sophie."

"What?"

"A snail. Every snail has a big flat sticky muscle under it that it travels along on. That's called its foot. Next time you see a snail crawling along, pick it up carefully and turn it over, and you'll see. There are loads in the garden."

"Come on! Let's find one!" said Matthew to Mark and Mark to Matthew at the same time.

"Wait for me," said Sophie. But they didn't, so she plodded after them.

When she caught up with the twins, in a far corner of the garden, each was examining the underside of a large snail. Sophie was not surprised to see that the snails were also obviously twins, the same size, the same shape, the same striped greeny-browny colour.

"I know!" said Matthew.

"I know what you're going to say!" said Mark.

"Let's have a snail race!" they said.

"How are you going to tell them apart?" said Sophie.

"I know!" said Mark.

"I know what you're going to say!" said Matthew.

"Fetch us a felt pen, Sophie," they said.

"What are you going to do?" asked Sophie when she came back with a red felt pen.

"Put my initial on my snail," said Mark and Matthew together.

"But you've got the same initial."

The boys looked at each other.

"I know!" they said.

"I know what you're going to say," said Sophie, and she plodded off again. She came back with a blue felt pen.

After a moment, "Ready?" said Matthew, holding up his snail with a big red M on its shell, and at the same instant, "Ready?" said Mark, holding up his snail with a big blue M.

"Wait for me," said Sophie. "I haven't got a snail yet," but already the twins had set their twin snails side by side on the path that ran between the edge of the lawn and the flowerbed. The path was made of big oval flagstones, and they chose the largest one, perhaps a metre long. The far end of the flagstone was to be the winning post.

"Ready, steady, go!" they shouted.

Sophie plodded off. "I'll beat them," she said. She was small but very determined.

Behind the first stone she moved, almost as though it had been waiting for her, was a snail. It was as different as possible from Red M and Blue M. It was very little, no bigger than Sophie's middle fingernail, and it was a lovely buttercup yellow.

As she watched, it stretched out its head, poked out its two horns, and began to crawl, very slowly. It had a most intelligent face, Sophie thought. She picked it up carefully, and turned it over.

"What a very small-sized shoe you would take, my dear," she said. "I don't know whether you can win a race but you are very beautiful. You shall be my snail."

"Who won?" she said to Matthew and Mark when she returned.

"They didn't go the right way," they both said.

"But mine went furthest," they both said.

"No, it didn't," they both said.

They picked up their snails and put them side by side once more.

"Wait for me," Sophie said, and she put down the little yellow snail. It looked very small beside the others.

"Just look at Sophie's snail!" hooted the twins, but this time when they shouted "Ready, steady, go!" neither Red M nor Blue M would move. They stayed stubbornly inside their shells and took not the slightest notice of their owners' cries of encouragement.

Sophie's snail plodded off.

It was small but very determined, and Sophie lay on the grass beside the path and watched it putting its best foot forward.

After half an hour, it reached the winning post.

Sophie jumped up. "Mine's the winner!" she cried, but there was no one to hear. The twins had become bored with snail-racing at exactly the same time and gone away. Red M and Blue M had gone away too, into the forest of the flowerbed. Only Sophie's snail kept stoutly on, while the straight silvery trail it had left glistened in the sunshine.

Sophie knelt down and carefully put her hand flat in front of the little yellow creature. It crawled solemnly onto it.

"You have such an intelligent look, my dear," said Sophie.

"What *have* you got in your hand, Sophie?" said her mother at tea-time.

"It's Sophie's snail!" chorused Matthew and Mark.

"Put it straight out in the garden," said the children's mother.

"No," said Sophie in a small but determined voice.

Her mother looked at her, sighed, picked up a box of matches, emptied the matches out and gave Sophie the empty box.

"Put it in there till after tea," she said, "and go and wash your hands."

All that evening Sophie played with her snail. When it was bedtime, and she was ready to wash and do her teeth, she put the snail carefully on the flat rim of the wash-basin.

Then (as she always did) she filled the basin with warm water right up to the overflow and washed her face and hands. The snail did not move, though it appeared to be watching.

Then (as she always did) she brushed her teeth very hard, making a lot of froth in her mouth and spitting the bubbly blobs of toothpaste out on top of the rather dirty water. She always liked doing this. The toothpaste blobs made strange shapes on the surface of the water, often like a map of the world. Tonight there was a big white Africa at one side of the basin.

Then (as she always did) she pulled the plug out, but as she turned to dry her hands the sleeve of her dressing gown scuffed the rim of the basin. Right into the middle of disappearing Africa fell a small yellow shape, and then the last of the whirlpooling frothing water disappeared down the plug hole, leaving the basin quite empty.

Sophie plodded down the stairs.

"My snail's gone down the plug hole," she said in a very quiet voice.

"You couldn't have kept it, you know," said her father gently. "It would have died anyway without its natural food."

"Next time you find one," said her mother, "just leave it in the garden. There are lots of other snails there, just as nice."

"Not as nice as my snail," said Sophie. She looked so unhappy that for once the twins said different things, in an effort to comfort her.

"'Spect it died quickly," said Matthew.

"Sure to be drowned by now," said Mark.

Try as she would, Sophie could not stop herself thinking about what happened to you if you went down a plug hole. She lay in bed and thought about the twins washing their hands in the basin and washing their teeth, and then later on Mum and Dad doing the same. All that water would be washing the body of her snail farther and farther away, down the drain into the sewer, down the sewer into the river, down the river into the sea.

When at last she slept, she dreamed that she was walking by the seaside, and there she saw, washed up on the beach, a familiar little yellow shape. But when she ran and picked it up, it had no head, no horns, no foot. It was just an empty snail shell.

Sophie woke early with the feeling that something awful had happened, and then she remembered what it was.

She plodded along to the bathroom and looked over the rim of the wash-basin at the round plug hole with its metal grating meant to stop things going down it.

"But you were too small," she said.

Leaning over as far as she could reach, she stared sadly into the black depths of the plug hole. And as she stared, suddenly two little horns poked up through the grating, and then a head, and then a shell no bigger than her middle fingernail, a shell that was a lovely buttercup yellow.

Very carefully Sophie reached out and picked up her small determined snail.

Very quietly she plodded down the stairs and opened the back door and went out into the garden and crossed the dewy lawn.

Very gently, at the exact spot she had found it, she put her snail down and watched it slowly move away on its very small foot.

"Goodbye, my dear," said Sophie. "I hope we meet again," and then she sat happily on the wet grass watching, till at last there was nothing more to be seen of Sophie's snail.

"Goodbye, my dear," said Sophie. "I hope we meet again."

A BAD BACK

Sophie was walking round the garden, wearing a pair of her mother's sunglasses. They were very dark glasses with a white frame. They made Sophie look like a panda. They made pink flowers look red and yellow flowers look golden and cabbages look blue.

Sophie walked along the path that ran along the front of the house and peered in through the dining-room window. Inside, everything looked very dark, the dining table, the chairs, the dresser with its rows of plates. The wood-block floor, usually the colour of milk chocolate, had turned to plain. But whatever in the world was that long shadowy thing lying on the floor?

"Yikes!" shouted Sophie. "It's a dead body!" and she galloped off down the path and through the back door and into the kitchen.

"Mum!" she cried. "There's a dead body on the dining-room floor."

"A dead body?" said her mother, busy stirring something. "I hope not, Sophie. But you're right. There is a body on the dining-room floor."

"Whose?" said Sophie in a strangled voice.

Her mother turned from the cooker.

"Goodness me!" she said. "You look like a panda. Take those things off. No wonder you couldn't recognize your own father."

In the dining room Sophie's father lay flat on the hard wood-block floor, his arms by his sides, and stared gloomily at the ceiling.

Sophie peeped round the door.

"Daddy?" she said.

"Yes."

"Are you all right?"

"No."

"What's the matter?"

"My back hurts."

"I'm not surprised," said Sophie. "Lying on that hard old floor. If you wanted to have a rest, why didn't you go to bed?"

Sophie's father sighed. "It's not because I'm lying on the floor that my back hurts," he said. "It's because my back hurts that I'm lying on the floor."

"Oh," said Sophie. She walked across the room and stood, feet apart, hands on hips, staring down at her father's upturned face with a worried frown on her own. "What have you done to your back?" she said.

"I don't know," said her father in a grumpy voice. "All I did was bend down to pick up a newspaper and something went *click*."

"And it hurt?"

"It certainly did."

"Does it now?"

"It's OK as long as I keep still and flat like this. It's the best thing to do, they say, but it's pretty boring."

Sophie lay down beside her father, her arms by her sides, and stared thoughtfully at the ceiling.

"Would you like to play a game?" she said.

"Not if there's any moving about in it."

"No," said Sophie. "We can play I-Spy. You'll only need to move your eyes. That won't hurt your back. Playing I-Spy will take your mind off it."

"Oh, all right," said her father. "You start."

"I spy," said Sophie, "with my little eye, something beginning with … *s*."

Sophie's father swivelled his eyes around the room. There was a row of saucers on the dresser.

"What have you done to your back?" she said.

"Saucer," he said.

"No."

He looked at the hanging light.

"Shade," he said.

"No."

On the wall there were pictures.

"Seaside," he said.

"You mustn't cheat, Daddy," said Sophie severely. "You can't see the seaside. It's miles and miles away."

"Yes, I can, in that picture."

"Oh. No, it's not that."

"I give up."

"You can't," said Sophie. "You can't just give up. But I'll give you a hint if you like."

"Go on then."

"Look above your head."

Sophie's father stared upwards.

"All I can see is the ceiling," he said.

"I knew you'd get it," said Sophie, "if you kept trying."

"Actually, Sophie," said her father, "*ceiling* begins with a *c*."

"How silly of it," said Sophie. "Well, then it doesn't count. It's my turn again."

Half an hour later Sophie's mother came in.

"Oh, I see you're being looked after," she said. "Perhaps you'll be a nurse when you grow up, Sophie."

"You know I'm going to be a lady farmer. Go on, Daddy, it's your turn."

"What are you playing?" said her mother.

"We're playing I-Spy," said Sophie. "I'm winning."

"I think you've won," said her father hollowly. "We've spied every single thing in the room. Why don't you run out in the garden now?"

"Oh no," said Sophie. "It's much more fun playing with you. I know lots more games. I'll just go and get some things," and she plodded off.

Sophie's mother smiled.

"Poor old chap," she said. "You're a prisoner. You can't escape."

"I don't know how much more play I can stand," said Sophie's father.

"You'll just have to take it all lying down," said Sophie's mother. "The longer you can stay there, the better," and she went out just as Sophie returned with her arms full. She was carrying paper and pencils, a draughts board and a box of draughts, a pack of cards and a set of Happy Families.

"There!" said Sophie, dumping them all beside her father. "That'll do for a start."

"I can't play all those games," said her father desperately. "Not when I'm lying flat."

"You can hold things in your hands, can't you?" said Sophie.

"I suppose so."

"Right. Here's a pencil and paper then. We'll begin with Noughts and Crosses."

At the end of a long, long morning, Sophie's mother came in again.

Sophie was sitting cross-legged beside her father. On her face was a look of triumph.

"Please can I have Miss Bun the Baker's Daughter?" she said. "And Master Bones the Butcher's Son?"

She pointed at the one remaining card. "You," she said, "must be Doctor Dose the Doctor."

Wearily her father handed over Doctor Dose. His face wore a look of great suffering.

"Is it your back?" Sophie's mother said. "Is it worse?"

Sophie's father moved his head from side to side on the floor.

"No," he said. "I haven't had time to think about it."

"We've had loads of games," Sophie said. "I won nearly all of them."

"Go and wash your hands for lunch, Sophie," her mother said and, when Sophie had gone out, "How are you going to manage? Can you eat down there? The doctor should be here soon. Hadn't you better stay there till he comes?"

"I . . . am . . . not . . . staying . . . one . . . minute . . . longer," said Sophie's father.

Very carefully, he levered himself to his feet.

Very gingerly, he took a couple of steps towards the door.

"It does feel better," he said in a tone of surprise.

"I told you so, Daddy," said Sophie, coming back. "I told you playing games would take your mind off it."

In the middle of lunch the doorbell rang. Sophie answered it. It was the doctor.

"Hullo," she said. "Is your name Dose?"

"Dose?" said the doctor. "No, it's Macdonald."

"Oh," said Sophie. "Well, come in anyway."

"What's this I hear?" said the doctor, coming into the dining room. "Trouble in this happy family? Done your back in, have you?"

"It feels a lot better now," said Sophie's father.

"Does it?" said the doctor. "Well, I can tell you one thing for sure, before I even have a look at you. There's only one way to deal with a bad back."

"There is?" said Sophie's father.

"Yes. The moment you've finished lunch, you lie down flat on it, on this nice hard wooden floor, and you stay there the rest of the day."

He turned to Sophie.

"You'll keep Daddy company, won't you?" he said. "Perhaps you could think of some games to play."

"Hullo," she said. "Is your name Dose?"

"Why," said Sophie, "do I have to wear a skirt?"

IN WHICH SOPHIE GOES TO SCHOOL

Every day of the two years that the twins had been at school, Sophie had always gone too, walking down with her mother or, if the weather was horrible, going in the car. But now, for the first time, she would not walk or ride home again at a quarter to nine in the morning.

Now, at last, she was a schoolgirl.

The day had not started well.

"Why," said Sophie, "do I have to wear a skirt?"

"It's part of the school uniform," her mother said. "You can't go dressed as you like."

Sophie's usual clothes consisted of an old blue jersey with her name written on it in white letters, old jeans and, most of the time, wellies.

But this morning she stood in front of the looking-glass and saw a distinctly grumpy figure wearing a grey pleated skirt and, under a maroon cardigan, a grey shirt with a striped tie.

"These clothes are mowldy, stupid and assive!" she said.

"You look very smart," her mother said.

"You look very smart," her father said when she came down to breakfast. The twins said nothing (because they had been told to say nothing), but they looked at Sophie, and then looked at one another, and grinned. Sophie eyed their grey trousers darkly.

"It's a pity you're not Scotch boys," she said.

"Why?"

"Then you'd have to wear skirts. They do. Aunt Al told me."

When they arrived at the school, Matthew and Mark galloped off without a backward look. Sophie and her mother made their way to the reception classroom. Here they found a number of other children who were starting school for the first time. Most were clinging tightly to their mothers, some were snivelling, and one little boy was wailing loudly.

Sophie's mother glanced anxiously at her, but her daughter's only reaction was to pull down her dark eyebrows in a frown of disapproval.

"Fancy crying!" said Sophie.

"Let's hang up your anorak," said her mother. "There are some pegs in the corridor outside. Let's see if we can find yours."

If there was one word that Sophie was confident of reading it was her own name, and she had no trouble in spotting it. Beside each peg a child's name was printed on a picture of an animal – a lion, an elephant, a parrot, a rabbit. Sophie's picture was of a black-and-white cow with a big udder.

"Yikes!" said Sophie softly. "They knew!"

Sophie's mother felt that this might be a good moment to slip away. She kissed her, and said, a little tremulously, "See you later."

"Alligator," said Sophie in her usual no-nonsense way, and plodded back into the classroom.

It just so happened that the reception class teacher was also beginning her first term at the school, so that all the children, new and old alike, were strange to her.

Mostly they were strange to Sophie too, as she sat where she had been told to sit and stared stonily at the others. Suddenly her expression changed from one of suspicion to one of active dislike.

Sitting on the other side of the room was a pretty little girl with golden hair done in bunches that were tied with ribbon. This child, whose name was Dawn, Sophie had met once before and an unhappy meeting it had been.

Dawn had been invited round to Sophie's house to play, and had deliberately squashed one of Sophie's largest woodlice. In return, Sophie had taken Dawn's toy pony, a pink pony with a long silvery mane and tail, called Twinkletoes, and had jumped up and down on it until it was a dirty squashed lump whose toes would never twinkle again.

Now, unaware of Sophie's sultry glare, Dawn chattered brightly with her friends, until the teacher called for quiet. Then she told the new children that each of them would have an older child in the class to look after them until they knew their way around the school.

"I know my way round," said Sophie.

"Do you?" said the teacher. "How clever of you ... let me see, you are...?"

"Sophie."

"How clever of you, Sophie. I expect you have an older sister in one of the other classes?"

"No."

"An older brother then?"

"No."

Sophie loved guessing games. "Go on," she said. "Try again."

"She's got *two* older brothers," piped up Dawn. "They're twins."

Unaware of Sophie's sultry glare, Dawn chattered brightly with her friends.

Sophie glowered furiously at her, but the teacher only said, "It's Dawn, isn't it? Yes, well, you seem to know all about Sophie's family, so you can look after her."

"Yuk!" said Sophie, folding her arms and sticking out her lower lip, while the smug smile on Dawn's pretty little face vanished abruptly.

When the bell rang for morning break, the teacher made sure that each new child had its escort before letting them go. Dawn, carrying a new blue pony, stood nervously before Sophie.

"D'you want to go to the toilet?" she said.

"No," said Sophie. She did – like mad – but she had already determined that she would do nothing that Dawn suggested.

Out in the playground, the whole school ran screaming and yelling and skipping and jumping. The twins came to make sure (because they had been told to make sure) that Sophie was not unhappy.

They found her standing in a corner, glowering at the madding crowd. Near by, but not too near, stood her minder, Dawn. "You OK?" shouted Mark, and, "You all right?" yelled Matthew.

Sophie nodded. Her expression, which was funereal, did not change.

The twins looked at Dawn, who was anxiously clutching the blue pony.

"What do you want?" they said together.

"I'm s'posed to be looking after her," Dawn said.

"She your friend?" said Matthew to Sophie.

"No."

"D'you want her hanging round?" said Mark.

"No."

"Well, get lost!" they both shouted, and off Dawn ran.

Sophie began to jig from foot to foot. Her brothers regarded her with practised eyes.

"D'you want to go?" asked Mark.

"Yes."

"D'you know where to go?" asked Matthew.

"Yes."

"Well, go then!" they both said, and off Sophie ran.

* * *

One of the Bad Things that had worried Sophie about Going to School had been Having to Eat School Lunches, especially pilchards in tomato sauce which she hated, and at lunch-time she plodded into the hall feeling sure that, today of all days, it would be pilchards. To her great delight, it was sausages and chips and baked beans, followed by apple crumble and custard, both favourites of hers; and not even having to sit next to Dawn stopped her from enjoying her lunch very much.

From then on everything seemed to improve, for in the afternoon they drew pictures to take home and show their parents.

Sophie loved drawing. She worked away with her coloured felt pens, dark head bent, tongue sticking out with the effort. All the other children in the class drew pictures of their mothers or fathers, or sometimes of their houses, but Sophie's was quite different from the rest.

"What a lot of things you're putting in your picture, Sophie," said the teacher when she came round to have a look. "What is it meant to be?"

Sophie looked at her scornfully.

"Can't you see?" she said.

"Well, I wasn't quite sure…"

"I'll show you," said Sophie, and with a red felt pen she wrote across the top of the picture in big wobbly capitals:

MY FARM

"That's *very* good, Sophie," said the teacher. "Fancy you being able to write like that, and spell correctly too! You're a bright one! D'you think you'll be a writer when you grow up?"

"Of course not," said Sophie. "I'm going to be a lady farmer."

* * *

"What have you got there, Sophie?" said her mother when she came to collect her. Sophie was carrying her drawing rolled into a scroll, with an elastic band round it.

"I did a picture," she said.

"Can I see?"

"When we get home, Mummy," Sophie said. "It's a present, you see. For you. And Daddy. And Matthew and Mark, I suppose."

"What's it of?" asked the twins.

"My farm."

"Your toy farm?"

"No, my real one, that I'm going to buy with my Farm Money, when I'm a grown-up lady."

At home Sophie would not undo the scroll, but waited till her father had come home from work. Then the whole family gathered round the kitchen table for the Exhibition of Sophie's Picture, the result of her labours on her first day at school.

"That's very good, Sophie," said her father. "'My Farm', eh?"

"No, mine," said Sophie.

"I was just reading out what you had written."

"It's beautiful," said her mother doubtfully.

But the twins were not prepared to leave it at that. They knew all about the animals that Sophie proposed to have, and they demanded to be shown the whereabouts in the picture of Blossom the cow and April and May the hens and Shorty the Shetland pony and Measles the pig.

There seemed, however, to be a great many more animals in the picture than these – dozens in fact, though it was anybody's guess which of the squiggly little figures were cows and which hens or horses or pigs.

"What are those?" asked Matthew, pointing to a group in one corner.

"Pigs of course," said Sophie.

"They look more like sheep," said Mark.

"Sophie's an impressionist," said her father, "and it's a great picture. But you seem to have got an awful lot of animals on your farm, considering that you're

The whole family gathered round the kitchen table for the Exhibition of Sophie's Picture.

planning to begin with just those five. How will you manage that?"

"I'll breed them of course," said Sophie. "Farm animals have lots of babies. I should have thought you'd have known that."

"Yes. How silly of me."

"What's this little black thing here?" asked her mother, pointing.

"That's Tom."

"Your cat?"

"Yes."

"And what's this brown thing over here?" said Mark. "Like a heap of something."

"It is a heap of something," said Sophie. "It's the dung-heap."

"Look," said Matthew. "There's a pair of legs sticking out of the top of it, as though someone had fallen in it head first."

"They have," said Sophie. "That's Dawn."

IN WHICH AUNT AL HAS AN IDEA

"Why were those cats making all that row earlier?" Sophie asked.

"Two toms, fighting, I expect," her father said.

"There's only one Tom – my one."

"All male cats are called toms."

"Why were they fighting?"

"Over a female, I should say."

"I bet my Tom won."

"I've told you before," her mother said. "He's not yours."

As soon as Sophie woke next morning, she jumped out of bed and went to her window. It was barely light, but she could see that there was a black cat sitting in the middle of the lawn, looking up at her window with his orange eyes.

Sophie crept downstairs and opened the back door, stuffing her feet into wellies. She hurried round to the lawn but the cat had gone.

"Tom, Tom," she called, keeping her voice down so as not to wake the rest of the family, and to her joy a voice answered, "Yee-es?" or that's how it sounded to Sophie. Out of the shrubbery he came to be stroked, and then he followed her back into the kitchen.

"Have some milk, my dear," Sophie said, and filled a saucer, which Tom quickly emptied.

"Now listen, Tom," said Sophie. "You can't stay in the house, they'd only get angry, so I'll have to put you out again. But come back tomorrow morning and I'll give you some more milk, understand?"

"Yee-es," said the cat.

And indeed it seemed he did, for from now on he was waiting at the back door every morning.

"It's a funny thing," said Sophie's mother at breakfast one day, "but we seem to be using much more milk than usual. I keep having to ask the milkman for extra. Are you boys drinking more than you ordinarily do?"

"No," said the twins. "We don't much like the stuff, you know that, Mum."

"Sophie?"

Sophie stuck rigidly to the truth.

"I like milk," she said. "That's partly why I'm going to be a lady farmer. But I'm not drinking more than usual."

All might have been well, had not Sophie's father needed to go to Scotland on business. This meant catching an early train, and Tom was just enjoying his saucerful and Sophie was enjoying watching him, when her father came into the room.

"So that's where the extra milk is going!" he said. "Sophie, get that animal out of here this minute!"

"But Daddy..."

"No buts. Out!"

"Come, Tom," said Sophie with dignity. "Daddy doesn't like cats."

"I certainly don't like somebody else's cat drinking our milk," said her father. "Cats are only good for one thing and that's catching mice. That cat does not come into this house again, Sophie, d'you understand?"

"Never?" said Sophie. She looked so woebegone that her father relented a little.

"I'll tell you what," he said, "if ever anyone sees a mouse in this house, then we'll think about having a cat."

"And don't think you can go putting saucers of milk out in the garden, Sophie," said her mother later, when she had heard all about it. "Cats should be given water

"Sophie, get that animal out of here this minute!"

to drink anyway, milk just makes them fat. And that cat's fat enough already." She should have known that Sophie, though small, was very determined, and if she had been about early enough in the days that followed, she would have seen that Sophie had no intention of giving Tom up. She did not let him in, and she did not give him milk, but she saw to it that there were scraps of some sort put out for his breakfast every morning.

Soon it was plain that Tom had forsaken his owners, whoever they were. Whether they were unworried by his disappearance, or whether they had moved house or gone to another district or abroad, no one ever knew, but the black cat had clearly adopted Sophie's garden as his territory and Sophie as his mistress. Now he even slept in the potting-shed.

Sophie was delighted of course. If only Daddy liked cats, she thought. If only we had mice in the house. But it was lovely to be continually meeting Tom in the garden, and lovely to be in bed at night and think of her black cat hunting in the black night outside.

"I bet Aunt Al will like you," she said to Tom. "Daddy's bringing her back with him, for a visit, when he comes home from Scotland. She lives in the Highlands, you know. They have Wild Cats there. Would you like to meet a Wild Cat?"

"Nee-o," said Tom.

When Aunt Al did arrive, apparently as fresh as a daisy after so long a journey, Sophie lost no time.

"Come and see Tom, Aunt Al," she said.

Aunt Al, small and birdlike with a sharp beaky nose, looked at Sophie with her head on one side.

"Who's Tom?" she said. "Your boyfriend?"

"No, that's Duncan," said Matthew.

"Tom's a cat," said Mark.

Aunt Al turned to her great-nephew.

"I thought you didn't like cats," she said.

"I don't," said Sophie's father. "And it is not allowed in the house."

"It's a stray," said Sophie's mother. "It seems to have adopted us. I've rung the police and the RSPCA but no one has claimed it."

"They have," said Sophie. "I have. It's my cat."

Tom seemed to take to Aunt Al straightaway. He came out of the shrubbery and wrapped himself around her thin bird's legs and made his steam-engine noise. Aunt Al scratched the roots of his ears.

"So you can't come indoors?" she said.

"Nee-o," said Tom.

"Only if we have a mouse in the house, Daddy says," said Sophie.

"Which is highly unlikely, I suppose," said Aunt Al.

The very next day was one of those lovely mild early spring days full of promise, and in the afternoon Aunt Al and Sophie were walking round the garden together. Sophie was carrying the yellow bucket in which she collected fresh creatures for her flocks and herds of snails and slugs and centipedes, to replace those who had decided to leave.

They came to the potting-shed, and there inside was Tom, crouching low.

"He's caught something," Aunt Al said, and sure enough there was a mouse between his forepaws. It was alive and, though bedraggled, apparently unharmed, but every time it tried to crawl away, Tom raked it back.

"Poor mouse!" Sophie cried. "Leave it, Tom!" But the black cat only growled at her.

"Cats eat mice, you know," said Aunt Al. "It's quite natural. He won't let you take it away from him."

"He will!" said Sophie. "I'll make him!" and she moved towards him in a most determined manner, swinging her yellow bucket threateningly.

With a cry that sounded remarkably like "Yikes!" Tom shot out of the shed.

With a cry that sounded remarkably like "Yikes!" Tom shot out of the shed.

"We can't just leave it here," said Sophie, looking at the mouse, so shocked that it was too afraid to move. "Tom will come back. What shall we do, Aunt Al?"

"Hang on half a tick," said Aunt Al. "Got an empty box somewhere? I've just had a brilliant idea."

Thus it was that, later on, Sophie and her mother and her great-great-aunt were having tea in the kitchen, when Aunt Al suddenly said, "What was that?"

"What was what?" said Sophie's mother.

"I thought I heard a little scratching noise. As though there was a mouse somewhere in the room."

"There are no mice in this house," said Sophie's mother. "I can tell you that for sure."

"I'm certain I heard it," said Aunt Al. "Listen, there it is again!"

"It's over in that corner," Sophie said. "Somewhere by that old cardboard box."

Sophie's mother got up from the table and went over to the box and lifted the lid. Then she shut it again quickly.

"Oh!" she cried. "It is a mouse! Oh, I don't like mice! Sophie, take it out into the garden."

When Sophie had done as she was told, she plodded back into the kitchen.

"Mummy," she said. "I told you what Daddy said, didn't I?"

"What?"

"'If ever anyone sees a mouse in this house,' he said, 'we'll think about having a cat.' So when Daddy comes back from work we can tell him we've seen a mouse, can't we?"

Sophie's mother looked at them both, the five year old and the eighty-one year old. Their faces were expressionless.

Hers broke into a big smile.

"You wicked pair!" she said.

IN WHICH SOPHIE GETS A SURPRISE

The twins' eighth birthday fell in late April, and Sophie was busy thinking what to get them.

"It's difficult, you see," she said to Tom, "to know whether to buy them the same things, which is a bit boring, or different things, when one might like his present more than the other."

She stroked his fat black stomach.

"What do you think?" she said, but he only purred.

She sought her father's opinion.

"I should ask them what they want," he said. So she did.

"What would you like for your birthday, Matthew?" she said to her elder brother.

"A radio-controlled model car," he said.

"And I want one too," said Mark.

"Oh," said Sophie. "What kind?"

"A Lamborghini," said Matthew.

"A Dune Buggy," said Mark.

"Oh," said Sophie. "How much do they cost?" she said.

"About £50," they said.

"£50 the two?"

"No, £50 each."

"Oh," said Sophie.

* * *

The twins' eighth birthday fell in late April, and Sophie was busy thinking what to get them.

She took her Farm Money out of her piggy-bank. There was Aunt Al's £5 note and quite a lot of coins that she had saved. She sought her mother's help in counting them.

"You've got 47p there," her mother said. "So that's £5.47 altogether."

"I don't think I can afford the sort of things the twins want," she said to Tom later.

"Nee-o."

"I suppose I could cut the £5 note in half."

"Nee-o."

Sophie rather agreed with him. She was not mean by nature, but that would have been over generous.

"You're right, Tom. It'll have to be the 47p. And it'll have to be sweets as usual. They like sweets."

So next time they went shopping, she told her mother that she was going to spend 47p buying sweets for the twins' birthday present.

In the shop, almost the first things to catch Sophie's eye were chocolate pennies.

"How much are those, Mummy?" she said.

Her mother looked.

"A penny each."

"So I could buy forty-seven of them?"

"Yes."

So she did.

Afterwards she said, "Mummy, what's half 47p?"

"Let's see … it's 23½p. Only there aren't halfpennies any more. If you wanted to split it, it would have to be 24p and 23p."

"Oh blow," said Sophie. "That's no good. They must have exactly the same number of chocolate pennies."

"Take one away," said her mother. "Then there'll be twenty-three for Matthew and twenty-three for Mark."

"Take one away? But what shall I do with it?"

"Open your mouth and shut your eyes, and I'll give you something to make you wise."

* * *

After carefully dividing the chocolate pennies into two heaps (she could count to twenty-three now), Sophie had then put each heap into a little cardboard box, had written the twins' names on each box, and then put LOVE FROM SOPHIE on both. The boxes were part of a store that she kept in the potting-shed, but Matthew and Mark were not aware that they had once been used for keeping black beetles in.

When the day came, they were delighted with Sophie's presents.

"Gosh, thanks, Sophie!" they said.

"That's all right."

"Must have cost you an awful lot," they said.

"It did. 47p."

"Open your mouth and shut your eyes, and I'll give you something to make you wise."

By chance the birthday was on a Sunday, which meant that the children's father was at home, and what's more, it was a beautiful sunny spring day. Matthew and Mark had each been allowed to ask three friends to tea, so they chose six boys with whom they regularly played football.

"Would you like to ask someone, Sophie?" her mother said.

"Darling Dawn?" said Mark.

"Or dearest Duncan?" said Matthew.

"Yuk!" said Sophie. "No thanks. I'll just have my friend Tom."

"You give that cat too much food," her father said. "He's as fat as butter. He needs to take more exercise. Which reminds me – boys, do you want to have the Olympic Games again?"

"Oh yes, please, Dad!" they cried.

The previous year their father, who was keen on that sort of thing, had organized all sorts of running and jumping and throwing competitions, and they had called them "the Olympic Games". There were races, short ones across the lawn and long ones right round the garden, and high jump and long jump, and throwing the discus (a tin plate) and tossing the caber (a clothes prop) and putting the shot (a brick).

So this year they did the same, and one or other of the twins, who were good at that sort of thing, won nearly everything, or else dead-heated for first place.

Sophie went in for every event and was always last because she was much the smallest, but everyone cheered her for her determination. And in the last race of all, the marathon, everyone had to run six times round the garden while Sophie was allowed to run only three times, and she won!

Then they all ate an enormous tea.

After all the guests had gone, Sophie plodded upstairs to play with her farm before bedtime. It had grown quite a bit since Christmas, for Sophie had either bought or been given a number of new animals, including a goat and some geese and a good few more cows. So big was it now that she had been allowed the use of the attic room at the top of the house so that the farm could be permanently laid out there on the floor. In the attic were some old bits of furniture and various oddments, and there was even an off-cut of carpet, grassy-green in colour, on which the animals stood or lay or grazed.

Sophie knelt on the floor, the black cat purring at her side. With one hand she stroked him, with the other she began to move the dairy herd.

"Time for milking," she said.

"Time for bed," said her father's voice.

He came in and sat down in a broken armchair.

"Come on, my old farmer," he said. "You must be tired, especially after winning a marathon."

"In a minute, Daddy, I've got to get the cows in first."

"In a minute, Daddy, I've got to get the cows in first."

She began to use both hands to pick them up, and Tom, released, jumped onto her father's lap. To her amazement, he was not only allowed to remain there, but she saw her father was actually stroking him!

"Daddy!" she said. "I thought you didn't like cats!"

"I don't," he said. "Except this one. I've got used to him, I suppose. You're a good boy, Tom, aren't you?"

"Nee-o," said the black cat.

"Oh yes, you are. Come on, Sophie love. Beddy-byes."

As soon as she woke the next morning Sophie felt that something was different. What? Oh yes, there was no black hot-water bottle on her feet. She got dressed and went out to see to her flocks and herds. There was no sign of Tom in the potting-shed, or anywhere in the garden, and stranger still, he did not appear at breakfast-time, which was when Sophie usually fed him.

By the time she had finished eating, Sophie was becoming rather worried, though she did not say anything to the others. She plodded upstairs to the attic to do the morning milking.

As she neared the door, she suddenly heard some faint little squeaks. They seemed to be coming from the old armchair. Sophie went to look in it, and then she gave a cry of "Yikes!"

In the chair, snuggling against the now much smaller stomach of Tom, were four little furry bodies. One was tabby, one was tortoiseshell, one was black with a white bib and white feet, and the fourth was coal-black, just like its mother.

"Oh Tom!" Sophie said. "How clever you are, my dear! And all this time I thought you were a boy. Whatever am I going to call you now?"

But the only answer was a loud proud purr of contentment from Sophie's Tom.

DOWN ON THE FARM

Sophie liked school. Learning things, she had decided by the end of her first term, was interesting, even though they did not have Farming Lessons, as she had hoped they would. But she could see that to be a lady farmer one day meant that you had to know how to read and write and do sums, so she set about these tasks in her usual determined manner.

Early in the summer term, her teacher was asked by the headmistress, "How is Sophie getting on?"

"Very well really. She takes a lot of trouble with her work. Wants to be a farmer, she tells me, so we do a lot of number work with the bottles of milk in the morning! Strange little girl though – lives in a world of her own."

"Still a bit of a loner, is she?"

"A bit. She certainly doesn't have a special friend in the class."

"Who's your special friend, Sophie?" her mother said one evening.

"Tomboy," said Sophie.

"No, I mean at school. In your class."

"Dawn?" said Matthew.

Dawn, pretty and fair-haired and always beautifully dressed, was the exact opposite of Sophie, both in looks and nature.

"Yuk!" said Sophie.

"Duncan?" said Mark.

Duncan was a very small, fat, short-legged boy with ginger hair. A one-time playmate of Sophie's, he had been "stolen" by Dawn while Sophie was away having chicken-pox. Both had paid dearly for this.

"He's a wally," said Sophie.

"Don't you like any of the children in your class then, Sophie?" asked her father.

"Not 'specially. Andrew's all right."

Her mother waited until Sophie had plodded off upstairs to play with the kittens, and then she said to the twins, "Who's Andrew?"

"He's new this term," said Mark.

"He's a farmer's son," said Matthew.

"Aha! Is he nice?"

"Dunno," they said. "We don't play with the infants."

In point of fact Sophie hadn't decided whether Andrew was nice or not – nor did she care. Once she had found out that his father was a farmer, she had determined to make a friend of him. Then, she thought, he would invite her to tea at the farm, and after a bit she would be able to go there often. She would be so useful to Andrew's father that he would ask her to come and help regularly – every day perhaps. And when she left school, she could work there. And, later, she and Andrew would probably get married and have four babies, just like Tomboy, and live happily ever after on the farm.

With such a prospect in view, what did it matter whether she liked Andrew or not?

Sophie took her time. She did not try to bribe him with sweets, as Dawn would have done, nor did she set out to boss him as she had bossed Duncan. Instead she began to ask Andrew lots of questions – about farming of course – whenever she just happened to find herself standing next to him in the playground.

Sophie's reason for this questioning was purely and simply to learn things that would be useful to her one day.

Andrew however, a sturdy little boy of about Sophie's height and build, but with very fair, almost white, hair, was flattered to be thought so knowledgeable, and answered these queries readily, if not always accurately.

"Your dad's a farmer, isn't he?" was Sophie's first question.

"Yes," said Andrew.

"I'm going to be a farmer when I grow up."

"You can't."

"Why not?"

"Farmers are men."

"Well," said Sophie, "I'm going to be a lady farmer. So there."

"I'm going to be a man farmer."

"You're lucky," said Sophie, "living on a farm now. Has your dad got cows?"

"Yes, hundreds."

"Can you milk them?"

"Yes, 'course I can."

"What else can you do?"

"Drive a tractor," said Andrew. He gripped an imaginary steering-wheel, engaged an imaginary gear, and set off round the playground shouting, "Broom-a-broom-a-broom-a-broom!"

Sophie stood waiting until he had completed a circuit, pulled on an imaginary handbrake and switched off.

"I wish I could see your tractor," she said.

But instead of the hoped-for invitation, Andrew only said, "It's green."

"How much did it cost?"

"'Bout half a million pounds."

"Yikes!" said Sophie. "Your dad must be rich!"

"He is," said Andrew. "And I shall be too when I grow up. I shall have six tractors and I shall have cows and pigs and sheep and chickens and ducks and geese and ..."

"...a Shetland pony?" said Sophie.

"Lots of them."

Each day now, at morning and afternoon playtimes, Sophie plied Andrew with questions of an agricultural nature. The fact that she monopolized his company did not escape the notice of her brothers.

Matthew and Mark prided themselves on being fast runners and, with the school's summer sports in mind, spent their time in high-speed dashes across the playground – in which, not surprisingly, they almost always dead-heated. However, they could not help but see that each time they hurled themselves against the chain-link fence that acted as a finishing line, there were Sophie and Andrew, dark and fair heads together, chattering away nineteen to the dozen.

"Sophie's always talking to that Andrew," they said to their parents.

"Why ever shouldn't she?" said their mother. "It's nice she's made a special friend at last, and he's a nice-looking little boy too."

"He's not my special friend," said Sophie. "He just knows all about farming, that's all."

"Must be a clever chap," said her father. "How old is he?"

"Five."

"Fancy!"

"Sophie fancies Andrew! " chanted the twins, and they ran off before Sophie had time to tell them that not only were they mowldy, but also both stupid and assive.

"Don't take any notice, darling," said her mother. "They're only teasing."

"It doesn't worry me," said Sophie loftily. "They only do it to be iterating."

"Don't you mean 'irritating'?" said her father.

"Both," said Sophie.

A couple of weeks went by, during which time Sophie continued her questioning. She was also made to move her own livestock from the attic to the potting-shed at the bottom of the garden.

"I'm not having those kittens messing all over the attic," her mother said.

"But they'll mess all over the potting-shed," said Sophie.

"And you'll clear it all up. That's what farmers spend most of their time doing, you know – clearing up all the muck their animals make."

* * *

"I'm not having those kittens messing all over the attic," said Sophie's mother.

"Your cows must make an awful lot of cowpats," Sophie said to Andrew the next day. "I wish I could see them."

"See the cowpats?"

"No, the cows."

"You can if you like."

"You'll have to ask me to tea."

"All right."

Sophie sighed. Silly boy, she thought, I'll have to fix it all myself, I can see.

"You ask your mummy to ask my mummy if I can," she said, "and then she can bring me."

"All right."

So at the end of the school day Andrew's mother saw her son approaching, his hand firmly held by a stocky little girl with an untidy mop of dark hair and a determined expression. Sophie's mother arrived in time to hear the ensuing conversation.

"Go on, Andrew, ask her," said Sophie.

"Mum," said Andrew. "Can Sophie come to tea?"

"She'd obviously fixed the whole thing up herself," Sophie's mother said to her husband. "I'd never even met the boy's mother before, but she seemed very nice. I said we'd pick Sophie up again about six."

"She'll have got herself into a lovely mess, I shouldn't wonder."

"Oh, I don't know – I made her take her wellies."

The phone rang in the hall.

Sophie's mother came back from answering it.

"You were right," she said. "That was Andrew's mother saying could I bring some clean clothes, Sophie is absolutely filthy. She slipped up and sat down in a really squelchy cowpat."

"Ah well," said Sophie's father. "Farming's just like any other job. Start at the bottom and work up."

At the end of the school day Andrew's mother saw her son approaching.

One day the twins came home in a state of high excitement.

ONE FINAL PRESENT

Before you could look round, it seemed to Sophie, those sunny summer holidays were over and the children were going back to school.

Matthew and Mark had nearly always gone off to play football with their friends, so Sophie had really only seen them at mealtimes.

It was much the same at school, except that now it was proper football with a proper pitch and goalposts.

One day the twins came home in a state of high excitement.

"What's up with you two?" their mother said. "Scored a goal each, have you?"

"No, Mum," said Mark. "It's the school concert."

"You know," said Matthew. "At the end of this term."

"We've got parts in the juniors' play!"

"I wish I could be in a play," said Sophie.

"You might be," said Matthew.

"The infants do one too, you know," said Mark.

"Who d'you think we're going to be, Mum?" said Matthew.

"Have a guess," said Mark.

"I don't even know what the play is," said their mother. "You'll have to tell me that first."

"It's all different bits out of *Alice in Wonderland*," said Mark.

"And *Through the Looking-Glass*," said Matthew.

"All put together," they said.

"You're a crazy couple," said their mother. "I should think you're going to be the Mad Hatter and the March Hare."

"No!" they shouted.
"I'm Tweedledum!" said Matthew.
"And I'm Tweedledee!" said Mark.
"And we're going to be all stuffed out with cushions …"
"… to make us look fat …"
"… and have a great battle …"
"… with toy swords!"
"Football and fighting!" said Sophie scornfully when the twins had run whooping away. "That's all boys think about."
"Perhaps you'll get a nice part in the infants' play," her mother said.

"Whose birthday is that?" asked the teacher. "Mine," said Sophie.

The very next day, as it happened, Sophie's teacher said to her class, "Now, after the end of this term, there's a very special day to look forward to. Who can tell me what it is called?"
A forest of hands shot up.
"Well, Dawn?"
"It's Christmas Day."
"And what's special about Christmas Day? Andrew?"
"You get lots of presents."
"That's not what I meant. Yes, Duncan?"
"You get a lot to eat."
"No, no," said the teacher. "Never mind about presents or food. Christmas Day is special because that's when we celebrate a very important birthday. And whose birthday is that?"

"Mine," said Sophie.

The teacher looked hard at Sophie. Then she opened her register and ran a finger down the class list of dates of birth.

Then she said, "Yes, Sophie, I remember now that your birthday is on Christmas Day. But I'm talking about a baby who was born nearly two thousand years ago, in Bethlehem."

Dawn's long skinny arm was raised.

"Yes, Dawn?"

"Jesus."

"Yes, that's right, good girl. Now you all remember the story of Jesus's birth, don't you? He was born in a stable, wasn't He?"

"Yes."

"They were full up in the pub," said Sophie.

"I don't think that's the right word to use, Sophie," said the teacher. "It was simply an inn where travellers rested. But yes, there was no room at the inn, so the baby was born in the stable and laid in a manger. What's a manger, someone? Andrew?"

"It's like a wooden trough," said Andrew. "You put hay in it. But we don't."

"Why not?"

"We make silage."

"Oh. I see. Anyway, this is what I want to tell you all. At the end of this term we shall have the school concert, and this class is going to act its own little play, all about the birth of Jesus. There'll be Mary and Joseph and the Wise Men and the shepherds and the innkeeper and ... now who have I forgotten?"

"The ox and the ass," said Sophie. "That could be me and Andrew, couldn't it?"

"No, Sophie, the animals will just be painted on the scenery. Now who will be the most important person in the whole play?"

"Baby Jesus!" they all chorused.

"Please, miss," said Duncan. "Can I be Baby Jesus?"

"He's small enough," said Sophie drily.

"No, no, Duncan, the baby will be represented by a doll. I couldn't have a live baby on the stage."

"You wouldn't have time," said Sophie.

"It takes nine months, like a cow," said Andrew.

Possibly these last two remarks had something to do with the fact that, when the leading parts in the play were allotted, Sophie and Andrew were passed over.

"Don't worry," said the teacher to those without starring roles. "You'll all be dressing up and singing 'Once in Royal David's City'."

"I'm in the infants' play," said Sophie that evening.

"Oh good," said her father. "Who else in your class is in it?"

"Everyone."

"Oh. What's it about?"

"It's an activity play."

"Don't you mean a 'nativity' play?"

"No, it's about Baby Jesus being born."

"Are you Mary?" said Mark.

"No."

"Who is?" said Matthew.

"Dawn," said Sophie.

"Yuk!" they said.

"Well, you can't be Joseph …"

"… or a Wise Man …"

"… or a shepherd …"

"… or the innkeeper …"

"… because they'll all be boys …"

"… so who are you?"

"I'm a crowd," said Sophie.

"Well, at least you won't have any words to learn then," her mother said.

"Except rhubarb, rhubarb, rhubarb," said her father.

"Why rhubarb?"

"That's what everyone says in crowd scenes."

Later, when the infant class had the first rehearsal of their Christmas play, Sophie and Andrew and the rest of the extras stood at the back of the stage, while Joseph and Mary and the innkeeper and the Wise Men and the shepherds were pushed and pulled into their proper places.

Mary – Dawn, that is – had brought in to school a bald baby doll of her own, and had beforehand been preparing to wrap its bare pink body in swaddling clothes, when Sophie had chanced by.

"That's no good," she said.

"Why not?" said Dawn.

"You blind?" said Sophie. "It's a girl."

"That's no good," said Sophie. "It's a girl."

* * *

But now Mary sat nursing the baby, Joseph standing proudly at her side, and on came the shepherds and the Wise Men bearing their gifts which they presented. But all the time no one said anything, not a word.

Sophie looked about at all the others in the crowd, but they too were silent. Sillies, she thought, they don't know what to say. But I do, and loudly she cried, "Rhubarb, rhubarb, rhubarb!"

"Anybody would think rhubarb was a rude word," said Sophie afterwards to an audience of two, Tomboy and Beano.

"Nee-o," said Tomboy.

"Well, the teacher got ever so mad with me, and I was only doing what Dad said. She's mowldy, stupid and assive, that's what she is."

Not long after the half-term break, Andrew said to Sophie, "Lucy's got puppies."

"How many?" said Sophie.

"Six."

"Yikes!"

"You can come and see them if you like."

Sophie hesitated. She longed to see the puppies, but she knew it would be awful because she would want one of them so much. Unwittingly, Andrew made matters worse.

"You could have one when they're old enough," he said.

"No," said Sophie. "They won't let me. Not till I'm eight."

"Well, d'you want to see them or not? Make your mind up."

Sophie made it up.

"OK," she said. "I'd better come to tea. You ask your mummy to ask my mummy if I can."

Sophie never forgot the first time she set eyes on that litter of six fat little terrier puppies. They were a fortnight old, their eyes not long opened, and they were just beginning to stumble about on their short legs.

All puppies are delightful creatures, especially to someone who is determined to become a lady farmer.

Lucy, the mother, was a smooth-haired small white terrier with some black patches.

"But the father of the pups," said Andrew's father, "was brown and white, so most of these have got some brown on them too. Which one do you like best, Sophie?"

Sophie rubbed the tip of her nose.

"That one," she said, and she pointed to a puppy that was all white except for a black patch over his right eye. "I just wish I could have him."

"Well, I'm going to sell the lot when they're old enough," said the farmer. "You'd better ask your mum and dad."

"They won't let me," said Sophie. "They say I'm too young."

"And how old are you?"

"I'll be six on Christmas Day."

"Will you indeed?" said Andrew's father. "Well, they're right. You are too young to have a dog of your own, same as Andrew here. Haven't your family a dog at all?"

"No."

"No animals?"

"I've got a cat and a rabbit," Sophie said.

"Ah well, you aren't doing too badly then. I dare say they'll get a dog one day. Come on then, Lucy – in you go with your pups. And Andrew and Sophie – it's time for tea."

With one last backward look at the white puppy with the black patch over his right eye, Sophie plodded off. I don't want to see them again, she said to herself.

"Which one do you like best, Sophie?" asked Andrew's father.

If Andrew asks me to tea before they're all sold, I shan't go. I couldn't bear it.

In fact, Andrew did not ask her again as November and the early part of December sped by, and soon the school concert was upon them.

Sophie's mother and father came with all the other parents to watch.

The nativity play went pretty well except that one of the Wise Men was silly enough to drop his gift. Sophie, wrapped in a red-checked gingham tablecloth and positioned at the rear of the crowd, remained silent, only mouthing "Rhubarb" when she caught her parents' eyes.

As for Tweedledum, he had the most tremendous fight with Tweedledee for stealing his nice new rattle, and, all in all, the concert was a great success.

Hardly was it over, it seemed to Sophie, than it was Christmas Eve, the eve of her sixth birthday. Christmas Day began as usual – the stockings, then breakfast, then the giving out of the presents, all stacked beneath the Christmas tree. Just before they started on that, the phone rang and it was Aunt Al, to wish them the compliments of the season.

When it was Sophie's turn to speak, she said, "How's Ollie?"

"He's fine," said Aunt Al. "He's grown. He's going to be the biggest cat in the Highlands, I should think."

"As big as a Scottish Wild Cat?"

"Shouldn't wonder. Have you had any good presents?"

"We haven't opened them yet."

"Hope you get a nice surprise," said Aunt Al.

As always, the presents were opened one at a time, youngest first. One for Sophie, then one for Mark, then Matthew, then Mummy, then Dad, and finally a birthday present for Sophie before she began again on her next Christmas one.

But this year, when all the presents had been undone and there was nothing left under the tree, Sophie's father said, "Now everybody stay put and play with your presents. I shan't be more than quarter of an hour," and out he went.

They heard the car start up.

"Where's Dad gone, Mum?" said Matthew.

"To fetch something."

"What is it?" said Mark.

"One final present."

"Who's it for?" said Sophie.

"All of us."

"For all of us?" said the three children with one voice.

"Yes. It's for Daddy and it's for me and it's for Matthew and it's for Mark and it's for Sophie."

The twins shook their heads.

"I don't get it," said Mark.

"Me neither," said Matthew.

As for Sophie, she suddenly remembered that in all the excitement she had fed neither Tomboy nor Beano, and she went off to give each a special Christmas breakfast.

No sooner was she back in the sitting-room with the others than they all heard the car returning.

"Sit still," their mother said. "Don't move."

The door opened, and in walked their father, carrying something in his arms.

When Sophie saw what it was, for once in her life she did not shout "Yikes!" because her throat had suddenly tightened up so that she could not have got the sound out. And for once, though she did not approve of crying, her eyes filled with tears. They were tears of happiness, at the sight of the puppy that was all white except for a black patch over his right eye.

The door opened, and in walked their father, carrying something in his arms.

"Yikes!" said Sophie. "Whatever sort is that?"

A NASTY SHOCK

In the summer term the schoolchildren went, once a week, to the local swimming baths, and by half-term Sophie had swum a width. She was not a graceful swimmer like Matthew and Mark, who could do a flashy crawl. Both twins were fast runners, winning all their races at the school sports, and swimming for them was just another form of racing.

Sophie, by contrast, sploshed along, using a stroke much like Puddle's. Puddle was the family dog. But she kept doggedly on, blowing like a grampus, determined not to give up. Just before the end of term, she swam a length of the baths.

She came out of school with a big grin on her face

"You look pleased with yourself," her mother said. "What have you been up to?"

"I done it!" said Sophie.

"Done what – I mean, did what?"

"Swum a length of the baths. I can swim properly. So Puddle can come with us to the seaside, can't he?"

The twins came racing up, dead-heating as usual.

"Mum!" they shouted in unison. "Sophie's swum a length!"

"She wasn't very fast," said Matthew. "She took ages."

"But she kept going," said Mark, "and she never put her feet down on the bottom once."

"'Course not," said Sophie.

She did not approve of cheating.

The whole conversation was repeated that evening, when the children's father returned from work.

"Well done, Sophie," he said and he looked at his wife.

"We can tell them now, can't we?" he said and she nodded.

"Tell us what?" they all said.

"Well, you see, the idea of taking Puddle with us complicated things a bit. Hotels and boarding-houses don't allow dogs. So we're going to stay somewhere where they do. It's only about three miles from the sea, so we can get to the beach in no time."

"And I think you'll all like it," said the children's mother."

"Especially Sophie."

"Why 'specially me?" said Sophie.

"Because we're going to stay on a farm."

Sophie's cry of *"Yikes!"* was the loudest they had ever heard. When her parents came to say goodnight to her that evening, she was lying in bed looking at pictures on her bedroom wall, the four pictures, drawn by her mother, of Blossom, of April and May, of Shorty, and of Measles.

"Will they have spotty pigs on this farm?" she said.

"Don't know. Perhaps. It says they have all sorts of different animals."

"Cows?"

"Probably."

"And hens?"

"Sure to."

"And Shetland ponies?"

"Don't know about Shetlands. They've got ponies. For riding."

"Yikes!" said Sophie very softly. "I could ride."

"You'll have to learn how to, properly," they said.

"I'll learn," said Sophie.

The final days of the summer term dragged by, but at last came the magic moment when the car was loaded and the family, and Puddle, were ready to set off for Cornwall and the sea.

"Don't forget my wellies," Sophie had said when they were packing.

"Wellies? On the beach?"

"On the farm," Sophie said.

Tomboy and Beano were to be looked after by a kind neighbour during the two weeks' holiday. Sophie had given strict instructions about their welfare.

"There's plenty of hay and rabbit-mixture for Beano," she said, "and what sort of bread do you have?"

"Wholemeal," said the neighbour. "Why?"

"He likes that," Sophie said. "The crusts. If you could spare some now and then? Lightly toasted."

Tomboy was to have the run of the kitchen via the cat-flap. "But," said Sophie, "she is to have water to drink, not milk, it makes her fat. But she can have as much tinned cat-food as she wants."

"Won't that make her fat?" said the neighbour.

"No," said Sophie. "It's full of protons and carbonhydrons, all different flavours, her favourite's Rabbit."

Now Sophie sat between the boys on the back seat, Puddle on her lap. He was nine months old now and as well-trained as small terriers ever can be, which isn't very well, as a rule.

He would walk on a lead without pulling, and come when called, and sit when told, but the command "Stay!" didn't mean much to him since he liked always to be on the go.

"He'll love the sea, won't he?" said Sophie.

"We all shall, I hope," said her mother. "Especially if this fine weather keeps up. Let's just hope it doesn't rain."

"Farmers need rain," said Sophie.

"Not while we're on holiday they don't," said her father.

"Or only at night," said her mother.

* * *

It was a long drive, and it was almost dark by the time they arrived, too late to think of going to a beach that day. But the farmer and his wife were very welcoming and they had a daughter of about Sophie's age called Jo.

When she was introduced, Sophie eyed Jo with some suspicion for she was quite a pretty girl, not unlike the dreaded Dawn to look at. However, she wore her fair hair short, and she had a friendly smile. More, she was wearing wellies and old scruffy clothes and she smelt quite strongly of pig, so Sophie was reassured.

Next morning, Sophie woke up early and looked out of the window of the funny little attic room that was to be hers and Puddle's for the two weeks.

She could see cows coming in for milking, and sheep in a field, and ponies in a paddock, and hens and ducks and geese in the yard, and she knew there must be at least one pig because of the smell of the farmer's daughter.

So she got dressed and tiptoed downstairs, Puddle following, and put on her wellies and went out. Jo, she found, was up already, crossing the yard with a bucket in her hand and a couple of collies at her heels, and she said "Hello," and the farm dogs sniffed at Puddle and wagged their tails.

"Hello," Sophie said. "Have you got pigs?"

"One," said Jo. "Just one."

"Is it a spotty one?"

"A Gloucester Old Spots, d'you mean?"

"Yes," said Sophie. "I've seen them. At the Royal Wessex Agricultural Show. I'm going to be a lady farmer, you see. Is your pig one of those?"

"No," said Jo. "I'm just going to feed him. You can come too, if you like."

So Sophie plodded after her till they came to an old-fashioned brick-built pigsty, and there was the oddest-looking pig she had ever seen.

It was a dirty blackish colour, and very fat, with very short legs and a short wrinkled neck and a huge stomach that almost brushed the ground.

"Yikes!" said Sophie. "Whatever sort is that?"

"He's a Vietnamese pot-bellied pig," said Jo. "He's my special pet. My dad thought up a special Vietnamese name for him."

"What?" said Sophie.

"Mee-blong-jo," said Jo.

Sophie, now also smelling of pig, ate an enormous breakfast, and then the family piled into the car and set off for the sea.

The beach was wide and sandy, with rocks to climb and pools to paddle in, and the sea was calm, and there weren't too many people about, and the sun shone in a cloudless sky.

They all swam, including Puddle, of course, and it was easier in the sea, Sophie found. Matthew and Mark went off with a football and in no time at all they had found some other boys and started a game. And Sophie's mum and dad lay in the sun.

Sophie made a sandcastle, except that it was really a sand-farmhouse, with a sand-cowshed and a sand-pigsty, and altogether everything was lovely.

"Happy, Sophie?" they said, and Sophie nodded.

I am, she thought. I like being on the beach and bathing, and I like my little bedroom, and Jo, she's all right, and Mee-blong-jo, he's mega, and I don't see what could spoil this holiday.

She got up from her building and called Puddle.

"I'm going for a walk along the beach," she said, "to get some shells."

"Not too far," they said. "Not out of our sight."

"OK," Sophie said.

She had not gone far when she came to a biggish rock that stuck up in the beach. Some people were sitting on the far side of this rock, a mother and father and a girl, and as Sophie approached, the girl got up and ran down towards the water.

She was a long-legged girl in a bright pink bathing-dress and her golden hair was done in bunches, tied with green ribbon.

It was Dawn.

ON THE PONY

Later Sophie took a piece of driftwood and went along to the big sticking-up rock, cautiously, in case they were still there. But they weren't, so Sophie wrote in the sand in huge letters:

Go hom Dawn

That'll scare her, she thought. She never saw me so it'll be really spooky for her to see her name there tomorrow; and at the end of the day Sophie went home much happier, while the incoming tide crept up the beach and washed out her message.

By bedtime Sophie had quite recovered her spirits. She had been allowed to feed Mee-blong-jo, she had helped pick up the eggs in the henhouse, she had spoken to some sheep and chatted to some cows, and finally Jo had taken her round the stables and showed her some of the ponies, for the next day Sophie was to have her first riding lesson.

"I expect my mum will put you up on this one," Jo said, stroking the velvety muzzle of a grey pony that was looking out over the half-door of its box. "She's called Bumblebee. She's a beginner's pony."

"She's got a nice face," said Sophie.

"She's as quiet as an old sheep," said Jo.

"She's as quiet as an old sheep," said Jo's mother the next morning as she saddled up Bumblebee.

Sophie's father and the twins had gone to the beach, while her mother stayed behind to watch the first lesson.

"Only one thing Bumblebee doesn't like," said the farmer's wife, "and that's pigs.

Which is one reason why we don't keep any, apart from that ugly old creature of Jo's."

"Why doesn't she like pigs?" asked Sophie.

A person who didn't like pigs would be foolish, she thought, so perhaps this was a foolish horse.

"Some horses are funny about things," the farmer's wife said. "We had a pony that was frightened stiff of the local bus – go mad, he would, if the bus came along. And another that hated going through gateways. Bumblebee, she can't stand pigs. Now then, Sophie, ever been on a horse before?"

"No," said Sophie, "but I'm going to be a lady farmer, so I shall have to know how to ride a horse round my flocks and herds."

"A lady farmer, eh? Not going to have a man about the place, then?"

"I might," said Sophie. "I might marry Andrew, but only if he's got a farm. If he hasn't, I shan't."

"You bain't so green as you'm cabbage-looking, as we say round these parts," said the farmer's wife. "Now then, let's get you up. You're not nervous, are you?"

"No," said Sophie. She was, a tiny bit, but she wasn't going to say so. All the same it felt very odd once she was sitting on Bumblebee's back. The pony was not a big one, but it did seem to Sophie that she was rather a long way from the ground.

Jo's mother showed her how to hold the reins, and how her feet should be in the irons ("toes to Heaven, heels to Hell"), and told her to sit up straight and to keep her hands low. Then she said, "Now, all we're going to do is to walk along nice and quiet, with me holding the leading-rein. Ready?"

"Just a minute," said Sophie's mother, and she got out her camera to take a picture of stocky Sophie sitting on stocky Bumblebee.

"Cheese, Sophie!" she cried, but Sophie's face was grimly determined under the hard hat.

"That cap I gave her looks a bit small," the farmer's wife said. "Jo's would fit her better, I think," and she called, "Jo!"

"Yes?" came a voice from the far side of the yard.

"Can you come here a minute, please? Quickly."

Jo was in the pigsty, scratching the bristly back of her Vietnamese pot-bellied pet, who had lowered himself a few inches to lie blissfully on his fat stomach.

"Stay there, Mee-blong-jo," she said. "Shan't be half a tick," and she ran out of the sty. She pulled the door to but did not bother to latch it. Slowly, it swung open again.

The procession had only just started out – the farmer's wife, leading Bumblebee, Sophie, now wearing Jo's hat, sitting as straight as a ramrod, her mother walking behind – when round the corner came the small, fat, bristly black shape of Mee-blong-jo, squeaking happily to himself at this unexpected freedom.

Bumblebee let out a shrill neigh of horror and shied violently, and Sophie came off with a thump.

Her mother rushed to her.

"It's all right, darling," she said. "Don't cry."

"I'm not," said Sophie.

Sophie did not approve of crying.

"Get that pig of yours out of here, Jo!" shouted the farmer's wife angrily, and to Sophie she said, "Have you hurt yourself?"

"No," said Sophie. She had, a tiny bit, but she wasn't going to say so.

"Perhaps we'd better leave it at that for today," her mother said.

"No," said Sophie. "I want to have another go."

"She's quite right," said the farmer's wife. She lowered her voice. "Best thing to do, get straight on again," she murmured. "Otherwise she might lose her nerve."

Sophie's mother smiled.

"Not Sophie," she said.

"Come on, then," said the farmer's wife. "Up we go."

"Can I say something to Bumblebee first?" Sophie asked.

"Of course, if you want to."

Sophie plodded round and reached up to the grey pony's head and stroked her nose.

"Now then, my dear," she said. "You listen to me. The P-I-G has gone, so there's no need to be frightened any more."

"I thought I'd better spell it," she said, once she was astride again. "You never know how much animals can understand."

"No doubt about it," said the farmer's wife to Sophie's mother. "She's going to be a proper lady farmer, she is. Walk on!"

THE RESCUE

Sophie's words seemed to have calmed Bumblebee, who was as quiet and sheeplike as you could wish for the rest of the ride.

Afterwards Sophie's mother found her standing with her back to a long looking-glass, peering round at her reflection.

"Whatever are you doing?" she asked.

"Jo's mum said I had a good seat," said Sophie, "so I was just looking at it."

Her mother laughed.

"She meant you sat naturally on a horse," she said, "and so you did. Some people ride like sacks of potatoes, but I think you're going to be a good horsewoman."

"Horsechild," said Sophie.

"How did you get on?" her father said when he came back.

"I got off," said Sophie.

"She fell off," said her mother, "but she got straight on again."

"That's my girl," said Sophie's father. "Small you may be, but determined you certainly are."

After that the holiday developed a pattern. Sophie had her riding lessons first thing after breakfast, and then they all spent the day together on the beach.

At first Sophie had tried to persuade them to go to a different, Dawn-free beach, but they said no, this was the nicest and the nearest and anyway with a bit of luck Dawn and her parents might go somewhere else.

Which they must have done, because although Sophie went off scouting each morning along the sands – in disguise, that is to say wearing her mother's dark glasses and with a sunhat pulled well down – there was no sign of them.

"She must have read my notice," said Sophie to Puddle.

Puddle was blissfully happy. Everything about the holiday suited him down to the ground. At night he slept in Sophie's room, supposedly in his basket but actually on her bed. Then there was the farm, with all its exciting sounds and smells, and his friends, the two collies. And lastly there was the sea, that lovely great watery paradise into which he plunged on any excuse and in which he swam tirelessly about, looking, with that black patch over one eye, the perfect pirate dog.

In general, he behaved very well, but he did have one bad habit. He would stand in front of anyone on the beach who was playing with a ball or a Frisbee, and yap at them.

What he was saying was as plain as could be.

"My family aren't throwing sticks for me just at the moment, so why don't you throw that ball or that Frisbee, and I'll bring it back to you and we can have a lovely game?"

Very occasionally some stranger would take notice of this request, but mostly people told him to buzz off, or else someone in Sophie's family would call him back to them.

But one morning in the second week of the holiday Puddle had wandered a little further than usual along the beach, when he came upon a girl in a bright pink bathing-dress, with golden hair done in bunches, tied with green ribbon.

Dawn was sitting on the sand, midway between the big sticking-up rock where her parents were, and the sea. She was playing with a Sindy doll that was almost a miniature of herself, bunches and all, and Puddle rushed up to her with a volley of barks that said, "Chuck it for me! Go on, chuck it, and I'll bring it back, or I might chew it a bit, it looks good enough to chew. Go on, chuck it!"

Dawn was terrified. She was nervous of dogs anyway, and now suddenly out of nowhere had come this strange, noisy, piratical terrier, whose mouth, every yap showed, was full of sharp white teeth. She leapt to her feet and fled.

For Puddle this all added to the fun, and he gave chase, bouncing like a rubber ball beside her and snapping at the Sindy doll, till Dawn, bleating "Mummy! Daddy! Help!" tripped and fell.

At this point Sophie appeared, plodding along in search of Puddle, only to see him apparently attacking a fallen child.

Then everything happened at once.

Puddle, trying madly to grab the doll in his jaws, suddenly received a hefty slap from Sophie and heard a furious shout of "Stop that, you bad dog, and get away!" and ran off.

Dawn's mother and father, rushing to the rescue, saw only that their precious daughter had been saved from a savage dog-attack by a stocky, dark-haired and apparently fearless little girl.

Puddle tried madly to grab the doll in his jaws.

And Dawn, once she had stopped howling, saw Sophie. Sophie's face was a picture. Fancy going to the help of that wimp Dawn! If only she'd realized in time she wouldn't have slapped poor Puddle, she'd have encouraged him. All he was trying to do was to chew up that revolting Sindy doll.

She turned to go back and make it up with the now distant Puddle, when Dawn's father said, "That was very brave of you, young lady."

"Brave?" said Sophie.

"Yes, rescuing my little girl from that vicious dog."

"He's not ..." began Sophie, at the same time as Dawn said to her mother, "It's Sophie. From school."

"Sophie?" said Dawn's mother in horrified tones, remembering their first meeting when, after the squashing of the woodlouse, Sophie had taken Dawn's toy pony Twinkletoes and solemnly jumped up and down on it until it was a dirty squashed lump.

"From the same school, are you?" said Dawn's father. "Well, well! It's a small world! Fancy you two friends meeting so far from home!"

"She's not ..." began Dawn and Sophie at the same time, but Dawn's father, who obviously liked the sound of his own voice, continued.

"Now then, young lady, we're very grateful to you for what you did. Our Dawn might have been badly bitten by that nasty, vicious brute, and so might you."

"But..." said Sophie.

"No buts," said Dawn's father, and he put his hand in the pocket of his shorts and took out two one pound coins and held them out to Sophie.

"Here," he said, "I should like you to accept these – they'll buy you a few ice-creams – and once again, many thanks for what you did."

"Yes, thank you," said Dawn's mother, rather unwillingly. "Dawn, what do you say to Sophie?"

"Thank you," said Dawn, very unwillingly.

Sophie took the coins. She opened her mouth and then shut it again. Then she said "Thanks" and plodded off.

* * *

Afterwards everyone fell about laughing when she told them what had happened.

"Dawn's father gave you two quid?" cried Matthew.

"For rescuing her from Puddle?" cried Mark.

"But surely he wasn't trying to bite her?" said Sophie's mother.

"No, he was trying to get her beastly Sindy doll."

"Tell us again," said her father, "what they called him."

"A nasty, vicious brute," said Sophie.

She cuddled Puddle.

"You are a very good boy," she said, "and I'm sorry I slapped you."

"Talk about getting money under false pretences!" said her father. "You really should have told them he was your dog."

"He isn't. He's ours."

"Well, ours then."

"I tried," said Sophie, "but they wouldn't listen. So I thought, well, that's another two pounds for my Farm Money. Every little helps."

"As the old lady said," added Matthew.

"When she peed in the sea," ended Mark.

"I could walk ten miles," Sophie said. "Couldn't I, Tomboy?"

SOPHIE IN THE GARDEN

One day in late autumn Sophie sat on the edge of her bed, holding her piggy-bank. She had just stuck a fresh label on its side. The first label, when she was only four, had said:

Farm munny
thank you
Sophie

Later, she had crossed out MUNNY and written MONNEY instead, and now, getting on for seven, she had designed a new label that read:

Farm Money. Please Give Genrusly.
Thank You. Sophie

Sophie unscrewed the plug in the pig's stomach and tipped out the contents and counted them. They came to twelve pounds, sixty pence.

She looked round the walls of her bedroom at the pictures, drawn by her mother, of a cow called Blossom, two hens called April and May, a spotty pig named Measles and a pony named Shorty.

These were the animals she would buy once she became a lady farmer. Sophie, though very small, was very determined, and no one in the family doubted that she would one day achieve her ambition.

Now she rubbed the tip of her nose, a sign that she was thinking deeply.

"Twelve pounds, sixty," said Sophie, "is not enough. I shall have to raise some more money, somehow."

At that moment Matthew and Mark burst into the room. Neither of them ever walked when he could run or spoke quietly when he could shout.

"Wow!" they cried with one voice, at the sight of the money spread upon Sophie's bed. "How much have you got?"

"Twelve pounds, sixty," said Sophie, "and where are your manners?"

"What d'you mean?" they said.

"You should knock before you come into a lady's bedroom. You're rude, you are."

"And mowldy," said Matthew.

"And stupid," said Mark.

"And assive," they both said, for this was how an angry Sophie had always described them.

They grinned at one another.

"I know!" said Mark.

"I know what you're going to say!" said Matthew.

"And so do I," said Sophie, "and the answer is NO. I am not going to lend you any money, not one penny."

"Meanie!" they cried, and off they dashed, racing one another down the stairs.

Sophie put all the money back in the piggy-bank and screwed up its stomach again. Then she plodded downstairs and stood it on the hall table, where anyone who came to the house would, she hoped, read its message. Then she went to find her mother.

"Mum," she said. "How do you raise money?"

"For a good cause, d'you mean?" her mother said.

"Yes. A very good one."

"Like Children in Need, that sort of thing?"

"Yes," said Sophie.

I am a child in need, she thought.

"Well, there are all sorts of ways. You can have jumble sales, or raffles, or things like sponsored walks."

"What's that mean?" asked Sophie.

"Well, people set out to walk a certain distance – ten miles, let's say – and other people agree to pay a sum of money for each mile they manage to go. Ten pence a mile, perhaps."

"Or one pound a mile?" said Sophie.

"Possibly."

"That'd be ten pounds."

"Yes, and if you persuaded ten people to sponsor you at one pound a mile, and then you walked ten miles, that'd be a hundred pounds for the good cause."

"Yikes!" said Sophie softly.

Ten miles, she thought. I bet I could walk ten miles. It's not like a marathon, you don't have to run.

Later she said to the twins, "How far is a marathon?"

"Twenty-six miles," said Matthew.

"And three hundred and eighty-five yards," said Mark.

Sophie went off to the potting-shed where once she had kept her flocks and herds of snails and slugs and centipedes and suchlike creatures. Now only her white rabbit Beano lived there in his large hutch.

Sophie discussed the matter with him.

"Just walking ten miles is easier than running more than twenty-six, wouldn't you say, my dear?" she asked him. "Miles easier."

Beano, a large rabbit with floppy ears, stared at her with his red eyes. He had a wiffly nose, and now he wiffled it at Sophie, in agreement, she thought.

Then Sophie's black cat Tomboy poked her nose around the door of the shed.

"I could walk ten miles," Sophie said. "Couldn't I, Tomboy?"

"*Nee-o*," said the cat, or that was what it sounded like. Sophie looked out at the garden. It was a rough square in shape, and there was a gravelled path that ran right round it. Sophie plodded right round it, once.

"I wonder how far that was," she said.

That evening she asked her father, "Daddy, how far is it round our garden?"

"Round the path, d'you mean?"

"Yes. Half a mile, d'you think?"

Sophie's father laughed.

"I'll pace it out for you if you like," he said. "My step is about a yard long. Why d'you want to know, anyway?"

"I just do," Sophie said.

So her father walked solemnly round all four sides of the garden, counting aloud.

"Eighty-nine," he said at the end. "Call it eighty-eight, it makes it easier, because then ten times round would be eight hundred and eighty yards, or half a mile."

"Yikes!" said Sophie. "So if you wanted to walk a mile, you'd have to go round ..." She paused for thought.

"Twenty times!" her father said.

"What if someone wanted to walk ten miles?"

"Two hundred times. If anyone was mad enough to do it. Satisfied now? Because I want to go in and watch the cricket on TV."

Two hundred times, Sophie thought. Still, I bet I could do that.

In the sitting-room she found Matthew and Mark, who were keen on all sport, also watching the cricket. Puddle sat in front of the television set too, quivering with eagerness. One thing he loved was chasing a ball, and he could see one there, being bowled or thrown or hit. Just let it come out of that box and he'd have it! Sophie stared at the screen absently, her mind full of this scheme – so simple, it seemed – for raising money.

Suppose Daddy gave a pound for each mile, and Mum another one, and the twins – no, more likely they'd give a penny. She'd have to get a lot of other people to pay, so as to raise a lot more Farm Money. Like everyone at school perhaps. Except Dawn, of course, who would certainly not give anything at all.

Still, the first thing to be done was to walk the ten miles. Then she could tell everybody she'd done it and then they'd pay up. First thing tomorrow, said Sophie to herself, I'll do it. Now, that decided, she paid some attention to the cricket. After a bit she said, "It looks nice and sunny where they're playing, so why is that man wearing a hat and a white coat and a sweater round his neck and another sweater tied round his middle? Is he cold?"

"No," they all said. "He's one of the umpires."

"The bowlers take off their sweaters to bowl," said Mark.

"And he looks after them," said Matthew.

"What a nice man," said Sophie.

A little later she said, "Why's he doing that?"

"Who?" said Matthew.

"The empire."

"Umpire," said Mark. "Doing what?"

"Taking something out of one of his pockets and putting it in the other one."

"Those are pebbles," said her father. "He's counting how many balls the bowler's bowled. When he's transferred six pebbles from one pocket to the other, he says 'Over'."

"Why?" said Sophie.

"It's the end of the over. Then everyone changes ends. They all cross over."

"Over what?" said Sophie.

"Oh, do be quiet, Sophie," said the twins.

"Just watch for a bit, Sophie," said her father, "and you may get the hang of it."

"No, I won't," said Sophie, and she stumped off, scowling.

By the time Sophie went to bed that night her plans were laid. First thing tomorrow she would do that ten-mile walk. Going round the garden two hundred times was sure to take quite a while, so, she thought, I must make an early start. She banged her head on the pillow six times, and went straight to sleep.

When she woke, she looked at her watch and saw to her surprise that it was indeed exactly six o'clock.

Sophie dressed quickly, crept downstairs, put on her wellies, and went out, Puddle at her heels, into a damp, overcast morning.

"We'll start by the potting-shed, my dear," she said to Puddle, "and when we come round to it for the two hundredth time, that'll be it. Simple. Except we'll have to keep count or we might go round too many times."

"Got it!" she said, and she bent and picked up a handful of bits of gravel from the path and put them in the pocket of her jeans. Then she opened the potting-shed door, said "Good morning" to Beano, gave him a carrot, and found an old cardboard box which had Baked Beans in black print on one side and on the other SNALES in big red capitals.

She put the box down in the doorway and set off around the garden path, Puddle following. As she passed the potting-shed after the first circuit, she took a piece of gravel from her pocket and dropped it into the cardboard box.

"Only a hundred and ninety-nine to go!" said Sophie to Beano, and plodded on. From the leaden sky a few large drops began to fall.

At half past six Sophie's mother was woken by the rattle of raindrops against her window-pane.

She got out of bed without disturbing her sleeping husband and went to look out into the garden. It needs rain, she thought. There below her was Sophie, plodding solemnly around the garden path in the steady downpour.

As her mother watched in amazement, she reached the open door of the potting-shed, took something from her pocket, threw it into a box, and stumped on, Puddle trotting after.

Sophie's mother hurried downstairs, threw a macintosh over her nightclothes and ran for the potting-shed through the teeming rain. Hardly had she reached its shelter than Sophie appeared again outside its door, a piece of gravel in her hand.

"Sophie!" her mother cried. "Come inside here straight away! "

Sophie came into the shed. Her dark hair, which always looked as though she had just come through a hedge backwards, now looked as if she had just swum the Channel. It was plastered to her head, and her clothes – old jeans and an old much-too-small blue jersey with her name written on it in white letters – were sopping wet. Her wellies squelched. Puddle, who loved water, came in too and shook himself happily over them.

"What in the world have you been doing?" Sophie's mother said.

Hardly had Sophie's mother reached the shelter of the potting-shed than Sophie appeared again.

"Walking," said Sophie shortly.

"In all this rain? Round and round the garden path? Why?"

"To raise money. For a good cause. Like you said."

"A sponsored walk, you mean?"

Sophie nodded, dripping.

"What were you trying to raise money for?"

"My farm," said Sophie. "I've only got twelve pounds, sixty."

Her mother looked fondly at her small but determined daughter.

"Come into the house," she said, "and we'll get those wet things off and put you in a nice hot bath."

"But I haven't finished my walk," Sophie said.

"Yes, you have. Come on."

"Oh, all right then," Sophie said. "Just wait half a minute," and she began to count the pieces of gravel in the SNALES box.

"Twenty," she said.

"You mean you've been round twenty times?"

"Yes. That's a mile, Dad said. I've still got nine miles to do."

In the bath Sophie sat playing with a rubber frog that squeaked. Puddle, rubbed dry now, sat on the mat hopefully. Just let it hop out of that bath and he'd have it!

"So how much money d'you think I'll get for walking a mile?" Sophie said.

"Sophie love," said her mother gently. "You've got things a bit muddled. A sponsored walk means that you have to go round to everyone *before* you do the walk and get them to sponsor you. *Then* you do the walk, and then they pay up."

"Oh," said Sophie.

"And usually people walk a long way across country, not just round and round the garden."

"Oh," said Sophie. "So I shan't get anything?"

"Well," said her mother, "let's pretend that I did sponsor you. How far did you say you'd gone?"

"A mile."

"Then I'll give you one pound."

Sophie grinned.

"Thanks, Mum," she said. "Actually I was quite glad to stop. I did want to do ten miles but I don't think I'd have had the stanima."

"Stamina, you mean."

"Yes. Can we have breakfast now? I'm starved."

"Why don't you say something nice to her, Sophie," said Aunt Al.

SOPHIE IN THE DOG-HOUSE

Sophie woke on Saturday morning and looked at the red circle round January the first. Today was the day of her first riding lesson – her combined Christmas and birthday present from Aunt Al.

"Happy New Year, my dear," she said to Tomboy, but the black cat only yawned.

Sophie looked at her watch. Seven o'clock. Only three hours to wait now. She got dressed and went downstairs to let Puddle out into the garden and to go to the potting-shed to feed Beano. Again she wished both animals a Happy New Year, but Puddle only barked at her because he wanted her to throw a stick, and Beano only wiffled his nose at her because he never said anything anyway.

At breakfast, though, everyone else returned her good wishes.

"This year," said Sophie's mother to Aunt Al, "Sophie will become a junior."

"Fancy!" said Aunt Al. "Do you look forward to that, Sophie?"

"Yes," said Sophie. "Then I can do judo and throw Dawn down on the mat."

"Who's Dawn?" asked Aunt Al.

"A girl in Sophie's class," said Mark.

"Sophie can't stand her," said Matthew.

"Why not?"

"She's a wimp," said Sophie.

She looked at her watch.

"Only an hour and a half to go," she said. "We ought to be getting ready."

"It's only a ten-minute drive to Cloverlea Stables," her mother said. "By the way, who's coming to watch Sophie's riding lesson?"

"I'm playing golf," said Sophie's father.

"We're playing football," said the twins.

"Aunt Al?"

"Wouldn't miss it for the world. Has she got a hard hat?"

"No," said Sophie's mother. "They supply them with a proper jockey skull cap with a silk over it."

"What about jodhpurs?"

"Jeans will have to do. I dare say some of the others will have fancy clothes but Sophie doesn't mind, do you, darling?"

"No," said Sophie. "All you need is a good seat."

"Attagirl!" said Aunt Al.

It was a good job that Sophie wasn't fussy, because when they arrived the three other little girls already there were rather smartly dressed. Meg Morris greeted them, and everyone was introduced, including Dolly, who came running up to rub against Sophie.

"We're just waiting for the last of the group," said Meg, and then, "Oh, here she comes now," as another car drew up.

Out of it stepped first Dawn's mother and then Dawn.

"Yuk!" said Sophie loudly.

Dawn was kitted out in skin-tight breeches, polished riding boots, a natty checked hacking jacket, and under it a silk blouse topped by a stock with a gold pin through it. She was even wearing a little bowler hat. She looked a perfect fashion plate. She also looked nervous, until she caught sight of Sophie, when she looked *very* nervous.

Dawn's mother also looked uncomfortable when she recognized Sophie's mother, and they nodded awkwardly at one another as Meg Morris took the five little girls away to introduce them to their ponies.

"Aunt Al," said Sophie's mother. "D'you mind if I just nip off to do some shopping? I shan't be long. I'll be back to see Sophie performing. Will you be all right?"

"Of course," said Aunt Al.

She watched as the five children returned, each leading her pony, and as Meg showed them in turn how to tighten their girths, pull down their stirrups, and then how to mount.

Four of them seemed quite at home in the saddle, but gawky Dawn sat awkwardly, shooting anxious glances towards her mother.

"Now then," said Meg Morris, "I'm going to walk right round with each of you in turn. We'll go on the left rein – that's anti-clockwise – from this post marked A, right round to the post marked F."

"All King Edward's Horses Can Manage Big Feeds," said Sophie.

"Well done, Sophie!" said Meg. "Fancy knowing that!"

Sophie looked pleased.

Three of the other girls looked puzzled.

Dawn looked pale.

As Meg Morris moved off around the menage with the first of the children, Aunt Al came forward to the rails to stand beside Sophie's pony.

"Sophie," she said in a low voice. "That girl behind you. D'you know her?"

"Not half," said Sophie. "That's Dawn, that is."

"She's nervous," said Aunt Al.

"Of course she is," said Sophie. "She's a wimp," and she looked round scornfully at Dawn.

"We can't all be brave, you know," said Aunt Al. "Why don't you say something nice to her, to encourage her?"

"You must be joking," said Sophie rudely.

"I am not joking, Sophie," said Aunt Al, and there was a steely edge to her voice. "If you cannot do a simple kindness, then though this is your first lesson, it may well be your last. I am not paying out good money for bad behaviour," and she turned away and walked off on her thin bird's legs.

Sophie went very red in the face.

Then she turned in her saddle to face Dawn, who looked, if possible, even more unhappy at this.

"What's the matter with you?" said Sophie gruffly.

"I don't like it," said Dawn miserably. "I might fall off."

Sophie looked at Dawn's long legs.

"Well, it isn't far if you do," she said.

"I'm frightened," said Dawn.

Sophie took a deep breath.

"Look, Dawn," she said in as kindly a voice as she could manage, "you'll be all right. There's nothing to be scared of. All you've got to do is sit there and the lady will hold on to your bridle. You can't come to any harm, honestly. And if you don't like it, well, then you needn't come back here any more."

And I hope you don't, she thought.

So amazed was Dawn to be spoken to by Sophie in such an almost friendly way that she quite forgot her fears and allowed herself to be led around in a daze.

Her mother watched, smiling.

Aunt Al watched, poker-faced.

Sophie's mother returned from her shopping in time to see her daughter being told to "Walk on".

It did not take Meg Morris long to realize that Sophie, for all her lack of experience, was a natural rider, and she treated her differently from the others, who watched admiringly, especially the now pink-cheeked Dawn. Soon she had Sophie changing rein, to go clockwise around the menage, and then it was "Trot on", with Sophie rising in her saddle to the manner born.

When the lesson was over, and Sophie plodded up to join them, her mother said, "Well done, darling, you rode very well."

Aunt Al said, "Well done, Sophie. Now you can look forward to the rest of your riding lessons."

She looked directly down at Sophie with her sharp blue eyes, and Sophie knew exactly what she meant, and they grinned at one another.

"She does ride well, doesn't she?" said Sophie's mother.

"Not bad," said Aunt Al. "Just needs a touch of the whip now and then."

SOPHIE AT THE FARM

Aunt Al's visit ended before Sophie's second riding lesson. They parted the best of friends.

"Mind you let me know how the rest of the lessons go," Aunt Al said. "I think you'll make a fine horsewoman."

"Horsegirl," Sophie said.

"Yes, but time flies, and you'll be a woman before you can say 'Jack Robinson'."

"Jack Robinson!" said Sophie quickly, grinning.

"And when you're a bit older, you must come and visit me and Ollie. You'd love the Highlands."

"Just me, alone?" said Sophie.

"Well, it would be nice if all the family could come, this summer perhaps – your father talks about having a Scottish holiday one year – but yes, I should like it very much if you came by yourself, once you're old enough to make the journey on your own. Say in about – let's see – eight years' time, when you'll be fifteen."

Sophie did a sum in her head.

"But you'll be ninety then," she said, "if..." and she stopped.

"If I haven't kicked the bucket, you were going to say," said Aunt Al. "Don't worry, Sophie, I have every intention of scoring a century and getting that telegram from the Queen. My father lived to be a hundred and two and three-quarters, so I've got form."

"Will Ollie still be alive?" Sophie asked.

"Don't see why not. He's still got all nine lives left."

* * *

When it came to the actual time to say goodbye, Sophie supposed they would shake hands, as they always had done before. Neither of them were great kissers. But as it was, she found herself flinging her arms round Aunt Al's skinny middle and burying her face against her, while her great-great-aunt stroked her tousled mop of dark hair. And as Aunt Al was driven away to the railway station while they all waved goodbye, Sophie shouted, "See you!" and Aunt Al called back, "Sure thing!" and then she was gone.

The following day Sophie went to Cloverlea Stables for her second lesson. To her relief, she found that Dawn had not turned up. She had not wanted to go on being nice to her, and now she needn't.

"Is Dawn ill?" she said to Meg Morris.

"No," said Meg. "She's not coming any more."

"Oh dear," said Sophie. "What a shame."

"I think perhaps she's not the horsy type," said Meg.

"No," said Sophie. "She wants to be a hairdresser."

She knew this because last term her class had had to write down what they would like to be when they grew up.

A lot of boys wanted to be professional footballers or racing drivers, and nursing or teaching were popular choices for the girls, though there were several, including Dawn, who chose hairdressing. Andrew of course wrote "Farmer" and Sophie "Lady Farmer".

Duncan wrote "Cook", and when asked why, said simply, "I like food."

At the start of the new term, Sophie tackled her father on the subject of pocket money. Due to the cost of the Christmas presents she had bought, her Farm

Money was now down to nine pounds, ten pence.

"I've been collecting for three years," she said to her father, "So I'm only making about three pounds a year. What d'you call someone who is really poor?"

"A pauper?" said her father.

"Well," said Sophie, "I'm pauper than anyone else."

She had worked out a sum on a piece of paper and now she produced it.

"Look," she said. "I want to have enough money to buy a farm by the time I'm grown up, which is eighteen these days, which is in eleven years and three times eleven is thirty-three, plus what I've got now makes forty-two pounds, ten. How am I going to become a lady farmer if I've only got forty-two pounds?"

"Perhaps you'll marry a farmer," her father said. "That's one way to do it."

"I am not marrying Andrew unless he gets his father's farm," said Sophie.

"When the father retires, you mean?"

"Or dies," said Sophie matter-of-factly. "He's quite old."

I shouldn't think he's forty yet, thought Sophie's father. About my age in fact.

"Well, you'll just have to save harder, Sophie," he said.

"I ought to be on Family Insistence," Sophie said.

"Assistance, you mean?"

"You can call it what you like," said Sophie. "I mean, more pocket money. I'm seven now. I ought to have one pound a week, like Matthew and Mark do. It's not fair. I get 50p and they get two pounds."

"But there are two of them."

"It's all because I'm a girl," said Sophie. "Women ought to be paid the same as men."

Sophie's father felt himself wilting before his daughter's determination.

"Oh, very well then," he said. "I'll put your pocket money up to one pound a week."

"Thanks, Daddy," said Sophie.

She consulted her piece of paper again.

"It's more than two weeks since my birthday," she said, "so now you owe me two extra 50ps already."

"Oh, Sophie," said her father. "You're going to be a businesswoman and no mistake.

Andrew could do worse. He'll be a lucky chap if he decides to marry you."

Sophie rubbed the tip of her nose.

"He won't decide," she said, "but you've given me an idea."

In the playground next day Sophie said to Andrew, "I haven't been to tea with you yet this term."

"It's only the second day," said Andrew.

"I still haven't been. You'd better get your mum to ask me."

"Oh, all right."

So a couple of days after that, Andrew's mother asked Sophie's mother if Sophie could come to tea.

"I'll try to keep her from falling in cowpats or into the duckpond," she said.

Before tea Andrew's father took both children to have a look at a sow that had had a litter of ten piglets only the night before. As they looked through the bars of the pen in which the sow lay nursing her already fat pink babies, Sophie said to Andrew's father, "How old are you?"

"I'll be forty this year," he said.

"When are you going to retire?"

Andrew's father smiled.

"Not yet awhile, Sophie," he said. "In another twenty years perhaps, when Andrew's old enough to take over."

"Oh," said Sophie. "He's going to, is he?"

"I hope so. This farm's been handed down from father to son for a long time now."

"I shall drive all the tractors," Andrew said.

"He's clever with his hands," said his father. "Makes some wonderful models with Lego. Should be good with the mechanical side of things."

"I'm good with animals," said Sophie. "I'm going to be a lady farmer, you know."

Andrew's father looked at the two seven-year-olds, one very fair, almost white-haired, one dark, standing side by side at the pig pen. Just suppose … in twenty years' time … he said to himself. Andrew could do worse.

"I'm going to be a lady farmer, you know," said Sophie.

After tea Andrew and Sophie were watching children's TV. At least, Andrew was watching. Sophie was thinking. Presently she said, "How much pocket money do you get?"

"One pound a week," said Andrew.

Sophie nodded. I was right, she thought.

"And how much money have you got saved?" she said.

"About two hundred pounds," said Andrew.

"Don't be silly, Andrew," said Sophie. "How much really?"

"I got twenty pounds altogether for Christmas that I haven't spent yet."

"You don't want to go spending it," Sophie said. "You want to save it."

"Oh, all right," said Andrew, who wanted to watch the programme uninterrupted.

"You ought to be able to save 50p a week," said Sophie.

"Oh, all right."

"And if I can do the same, well, in twenty years' time we'll have a nice lot between us. And then I shan't have to buy a farm and the animals will all be here already and your dad can have a nice rest and you'll be the farmer and I'll be the lady farmer."

Andrew, glued to the screen, did not answer.

Sophie sighed.

"Andrew," she said, "listen to me."

"What?"

"When we're grown up, I'm going to marry you."

"Oh, all right."

That evening, when Sophie's parents came to her bedroom to say goodnight, she was looking, they thought, particularly happy. Tomboy, lying on her feet, was purring loudly.

"What's up with you?" her mother said. "You look like the cat that's eaten the cream."

"They look like two cats," her father said, "that have eaten two lots of cream."

"Well," said Sophie, "I've something to tell you. I'll write to Aunt Al and tell her, but don't say anything to the boys, they wouldn't understand."

"Understand what?" they said. "What is it you've got to tell us?"

Sophie sat up in bed.

"I wanted you to be the first to know," she said. "I'm engaged."

"You, my dear," said Sophie to Beano, "are looking too fat."

IN WHICH SOPHIE IS BOWLED OVER

Sophie and her family were going to Scotland for a summer holiday, to stay with Aunt Al. Sophie of course told both Tomboy and Puddle about the coming trip. Tomboy, she felt sure, would be interested because of Ollie.

"I'll give him your love, my dear, never fear," said Sophie.

Puddle was to be taken with them. Sophie had been at her most determined about this.

"If he doesn't go, then I don't go," she said to her parents. "You'll have to put me in kennels too."

She had tried to interest Beano in the news (he had, after all, been a gift from Aunt Al), but the big white rabbit just gazed blankly at her with his pink eyes. Not for one moment would Sophie have allowed that Beano was stupid, but conversation with him tended to be one-sided.

Tomboy usually purred or mewed in reply to what she had to say, and Puddle wagged, or indeed barked, if she used an excited tone of voice. But Beano just wiffled his nose.

To make up for his silence, Sophie always talked to him a great deal.

One Saturday afternoon she spent a long time in the potting-shed, giving Beano's hutch a specially thorough clean, and chattering busily away to him as he pottered about the floor.

When all was ready – his water-bottle and his hay-rack filled, his rabbit-mixture in his feeding-bowl with a nice carrot beside it, the hutch floor carpeted with fresh sawdust – Sophie stood, hands on hips, regarding her rabbit with the critical eye of a would-be lady farmer.

"You, my dear," she said, "are looking too fat. You haven't had enough exercise lately."

When Beano had first arrived, Sophie had tried exercising him on a lead. She had bought, out of her Farm Money, a smart blue collar and lead, originally for Tomboy (who didn't care for this), and in summertime she would drop the loop of the lead over a stake driven into the lawn, and Beano would graze happily round it in a circle. On the arrival of Puddle, Sophie had sold the collar and lead back to the family (for Puddle was the family's dog, not hers alone) for a profit.

"We'll borrow them back," said Sophie now to Beano. "Puddle won't mind lending them. And then I'm going to take you for a nice long walk in the garden, before it gets too dark."

In fact, taking Beano for a walk meant being taken for a walk by Beano, who was only interested in going his own way. The big rabbit was strong, and he towed Sophie about the garden, to the amusement of Matthew and Mark, who were still, in the fading light, playing one-a-side football on the lawn: two bamboo poles were stuck in the grass at either end, as goals.

Suddenly, Beano took it into his head to try to run across the pitch, while Sophie hauled on his lead to no avail.

At the same time one of the boys took a shot at goal, and the ball struck Sophie full on the side of her head. Dazed, she fell to her knees, letting go of the lead.

"Gosh, sorry, Sophie!" the kicker cried, and "He didn't mean to!" cried his opponent, and they both squatted anxiously beside their sister.

"Don't cry," they said.

"I'm not," said Sophie.

Sophie did not approve of crying.

"Are you all right?" they said.

Sophie shook her head.

"I feel a bit dizzy," she said.

"You better come inside," said Mark.

The ball struck Sophie full on the side of her head.

"And sit down for a bit," said Matthew, and they each took one of Sophie's arms and raised her up and marched her off the pitch.

"Mum!" they shouted. "Sophie's injured!"

Then they explained what had happened, and Mark said that it was he who had kicked the ball, and Matthew said that Mark hadn't meant to hurt Sophie, and Sophie said she had a bit of a headache, and their mother said that Sophie had better lie down on the sofa for a bit.

Which she did.

But after a while she suddenly remembered – Beano! She'd dropped the lead when the ball hit her. Beano was still out, in the dark garden.

"Quick!" she shouted, leaping to her feet. "We must find him!"

"Find who?" they all said.

"My rabbit. He's loose in the garden!" cried Sophie, and she rushed out.

"Go with her, boys," their mother said, "while I make sure the gate into the road is shut, and then I'll come and help you look."

By now it was quite dark, and though they all searched for ages with a torch – over the lawn, in the flower-beds, in the vegetable patch and through the shrubbery – there was no sign of Beano.

"Perhaps he's hopped back into the potting-shed," said Sophie's mother. But he hadn't. There in the torchlight was his hutch, beautifully clean but quite empty. He had simply disappeared.

"The gate was shut, wasn't it, Mum?" said Sophie.

"Yes."

"He must be somewhere in the garden," Sophie said.

"Of course he is. We'll find him, don't worry. Let's all go and have some tea now – it's getting rather cold out here – and then we'll have another search and I expect he'll have come out from wherever he's hiding."

Sophie would not eat any tea.

"I couldn't," she said. "Not when Beano hasn't had his."

Afterwards all five of them – for the children's father had returned from the

Golf Club – put on coats (it was beginning to freeze) and mounted another search, but in vain.

At last they gave up – at least, four of them did. Sophie plodded doggedly on, prepared to go on all night if needs be. But, for once, her parents proved more determined than she was and insisted that she go to bed.

"There's nothing more we can do tonight," they said. "You snuggle down and go to sleep now, there's a good girl."

"I couldn't," Sophie said. "Not while Beano's out in the cold."

For a long time she didn't, but then at last, tired out, she fell deeply asleep.

Sophie woke early the following morning with the feeling that something was terribly wrong, and then she remembered and jumped out of bed and ran to the window.

It was just growing light, and the lawn, she could see, was white with frost. But on it there was no large white lolloping shape. Nothing stirred in the garden below, except – what was that?

Something was moving, along the top of the garden wall, some animal, the size of a small dog or a large cat. It walked along the wall and then stopped and sat there, looking down towards the potting-shed. It was reddish in colour, Sophie could see now as the light grew stronger, with a sharp pointed face and a bushy tail. It was a fox!

Before Sophie could think what to do, another animal appeared, a white one. Out from beneath the potting-shed, under which he had burrowed last evening to spend a comfortable night, emerged Beano. He hopped out on to the lawn, the blue collar around his neck, the blue lead trailing behind him, and sniffed curiously at the frosted grass. Each hop took him nearer to the watching fox.

"Look out, Beano, look out!" yelled Sophie at the top of her voice, but the double-glazing of her window deadened the sound, as the fox slipped down from the wall top, eyes fixed upon the approaching rabbit.

At that instant a third animal appeared upon the scene: a black animal, an angry animal, furious at the sight and the rank smell of this red bushy-tailed intruder into her garden.

Tomboy's ears were flat upon her head, her back arched, her coat stood on end, and suddenly she launched herself, spitting and yowling, straight at the fox, which turned tail and leaped back over the wall and was gone.

Matthew and Mark had slept through Sophie's loud shout, but it had woken her mother and father from their Sunday morning lie-in, and now they looked from their window to see Sophie, in dressing-gown and slippers, being towed by Beano back to the potting-shed and his nice clean hutch and his supper-become-breakfast.

Behind them, her tail raised high in triumph, her coat very black against the frosty grass, stalked Sophie's victorious Tomboy.

IN WHICH SOPHIE WINS A PRIZE

"Daddy and I had our honeymoon in Scotland, and we went to visit Aunt Al while we were there. We walked round the farm," said Sophie's mother.

"What farm?" said Sophie.

"Hers."

"She never told me she was a lady farmer," said Sophie.

"She isn't," her mother said. "The land belongs to her but it is let out to a neighbouring farmer. In the old days, Aunt Al's father used to breed Highland cattle, I believe."

"I've seen pictures of them! They've got long tously hair," said shaggy Sophie, "and long horns, and they're a lovely goldy colour."

"That's right."

"How big is the farm?" said Sophie.

"I don't really know. Smallish for Scotland, I think."

"How long is it before we go to Scotland?"

"Oh, goodness, it's more than three months away. You'll just have to be patient. Remember the old rhyme,

Patience is a Virtue.
Virtue is a Grace.
Grace is a little girl
Who wouldn't wash her face."

Grace sounded much nicer than Dawn, Sophie thought. Dawn was probably always washing her face.

She rubbed the tip of her nose.

"Mum," she said, "when I'm old enough, d'you think Aunt Al would let the farm to me?"

"Sophie, my love," her mother said, "you're not eight yet, and Aunt Al's going to be eighty-three in the autumn. So if you're talking about when you're twenty, let's say, then Aunt Al would be – let me see – ninety-five!"

"That's OK," said Sophie. "She told me she's going to live to be a hundred."

When the Easter holidays began, Sophie was not slow to remind her mother of her promise to pay for her to have a ride at Meg Morris' stables. Before breakfast on the very first morning she said, "Will you be ringing up the stables today?"

"The stables?"

"Yes. Cloverlea Stables. *You* know."

"Oh yes, of course," said her mother, and after breakfast she did. Sophie did not listen to her mother talking on the telephone. She sat in another room with her fingers crossed, and only when she heard the *ting!* as her mother rang off did she go to her and say, "Well?"

"Well," said Sophie's mother, "Meg's a bit busy at the moment, organizing an 'Own-a-Pony-Day'."

"What's that?" said Sophie.

"It's a whole day event that she runs – first a grooming competition, then a treasure hunt on foot, then a quiz, then a riding lesson, and then in the afternoon, after a picnic lunch, there's a gymkhana. It would be a lucky child who had all that, wouldn't it?"

"It would," said Sophie.

"Well, you're a lucky child."

"Yikes!" shouted Sophie. "Wicked! Mummy, you're ace!"

When "Own-a-Pony-Day" came, Sophie had a marvellous time. There were nine other girls and three boys, and Meg Morris gave them each a number to wear. Sophie was Number Thirteen.

She certainly didn't have any luck in the morning. Some of the other children were quite a bit older, and could reach higher up their ponies when grooming them, and run faster in the treasure hunt on foot, and answer harder questions in the quiz.

But in the afternoon it was different...

Back home afterwards, everyone wanted to know how well Sophie had done.

"Did you win a prize?" asked Mark.

Sophie nodded.

"What for?" asked Matthew.

"Gymkhana," said Sophie.

"Jim Carner?" they said. "Who's he?"

"It's a sort of a sports event on horseback," their mother said.

"What did you win?" asked Sophie's father.

"Oh, just a rosette," said Sophie off-handedly.

"Oh. What colour was it?"

"What does it matter what colour it was?" asked the twins.

"There are different ones, for first, second, third or fourth prize. I can't remember exactly which is which," said Sophie's father. "Tell us, Sophie."

"Green is for fourth place," Sophie said. "Yellow is for third. Blue is for second. And red is for first."

"Well, go on, tell us," everyone said. "What colour was yours?" and Sophie, grinning all over her face, drew from her pocket a red rosette.

* * *

Sophie's springtime triumph on "Own-a-Pony-Day" was matched, in midsummer, by the twins' customary successes on the school's Sports Day. Matthew and Mark were forever racing one another, and as usual they beat the other boys in most of the races.

Sophie was not much good at running, though once, when she was five, she had won the Infants' Egg-and-Spoon Race. This year she didn't win anything (though she tried hard enough), but she didn't mind too much. To have won that red rosette at the gymkhana had been enough. She had fixed it to her bedroom wall with Blu-Tack, underneath the picture of Shorty.

"I'm sorry, my dears," she said to Blossom, April, May and Measles, "but it has to go with a horse, even though it is rather a short horse."

Anyway, Sophie's mind hadn't really been on Sports Day. All she could think about was that in a week's time the summer term would be over at long last, and then they would all be setting off to stay with Aunt Al.

As the day of departure drew near, the children's father got out his motoring atlas to show them where they were going.

"It's a heck of a long way," he said. "It'll take us a couple of days."

"How far is it?" they said.

"About six hundred miles."

"If you went at sixty miles an hour …" said Matthew.

"… we'd be there in ten hours," said Mark.

Sophie watched her father's finger tracing the route on the map, from quite near the bottom of England to quite near the top of Scotland.

"Don't be silly," she said to her brothers. "You can't go up to Scotland at sixty miles an hour. Can't you see – it's uphill, all the way to the top of the Highlands."

"It's not," they said. "It's just going from south to north."

"Exactly," said Sophie. "Going up. After all, you wouldn't say 'I'm going *down* to the North Pole', would you?"

No amount of explanation would change Sophie's mind about this, and when they did set off on the long drive, she remarked at regular intervals that it would be better on the return journey, they'd be going downhill all the way.

In fact, when at last the family arrived at Balnacraig, Sophie was fast asleep in her seatbelt.

"Wake up, Sophie!" they all said. "We're here."

Sophie opened her eyes to see that they had drawn up on a sweep of gravel before a tall grey house. It had a great many long narrow windows and, above a flight of stone steps, a massive oak front door, which now opened to show a familiar small figure.

A massive oak front door opened to show a familiar small figure.

Aunt Al came down the steps on her thin bird's legs to greet them all – the grown-ups with a kiss, the boys with a hug. She came to Sophie last, looking, with her sharp blue eyes and her thin beaky nose, more birdlike than ever, and, knowing Sophie, attempted neither kiss nor hug, but held out her hand, bony and curled like a bird's claw. Sophie took it.

"How de do, Sophie?" said Aunt Al, and, "I'm very well," said Sophie and they grinned at one another.

The children spent the rest of that first day exploring the many tall dark rooms of the old house, right up to the attics that ran the length of it beneath its steep slate roof, decorated with many strange turrets and battlements.

Then there was the stable block, with its clock tower above, and inside, a double row of stabling divided by wooden partitions topped by iron rails.

On some of the doors, names were still dimly visible – MAJOR, STARLIGHT, DUCHESS – and on one, Sophie saw with delight, was written FRISK, the name of the pony that Aunt Al had owned when she was young. There were no horses within now, no stamp of hooves upon the cobbled floor, but the smell was still there, Sophie thought, a faint smell of horse and hay and harness.

Last thing that night, Aunt Al came up to say goodnight, in the little attic bedroom which was to be Sophie's for the holiday, and Sophie said to her, "You never told me you were a lady farmer."

"Well, I'm not, strictly speaking," said Aunt Al. "The land that I own is let out to a neighbouring farmer, Mr Grant."

"How much land?" said Sophie.

"Not a lot. Just over a hundred and fifty acres."

"Yikes!" said Sophie softly. "That's a lot. Can we go and see it tomorrow?"

"If you like."

"Just you and me?"

"I dare say it will be just you and me," said Aunt Al. "I know your mother is looking forward to taking things easy and putting her feet up a bit, and your father will want to go down to the loch."

"Loch Ness?"

"No, no, just a wee lochan, but there are fish to be had and I know he's keen to teach Matthew and Mark how to handle a rod. So you and I will walk down to the farm and see Mr Grant."

And after breakfast next morning they did.

Mr Grant was big and Mrs Grant was small and both of them had the sort of smiling faces that made Sophie like them straight away.

"This is my great-great-niece," Aunt Al said.

"She has a wee bit of a look of you about her, Miss Alice," said Mrs Grant. "Maybe not the features so much, but the expression. A determined person, I'd say."

"You'd be right," said Aunt Al, and to Mr Grant she said, "Is Lucky ready?"

"He is," said Mr Grant, and he went off across the yard.

"Who's Lucky?" said Sophie.

"He belongs to Mr and Mrs Grant's daughter," said Aunt Al, "but she's grown out of him, and they've very kindly agreed to lend him to you while you're here. Look."

And Sophie looked and saw the farmer leading out a stocky brown pony that looked as if it had just come through a hedge backwards.

"Here comes the horsegirl," said Aunt Al.

As a delighted Sophie stood at his head, patting him and telling him what a fine fellow he was, there was quite a likeness between them.

"His coat's in a mess, Miss Alice," said Mr Grant. "He wants grooming badly. But you told me that…"

"I told you," said Aunt Alice, "that if Sophie's going to ride him, then she's going to groom him. OK, Sophie?"

"OK!" said Sophie, and to the farmer she said, "Please, I shall want some warm water and a body-brush and a curry-comb and a dandy brush," and she grabbed Lucky's halter and said, "Walk on!" in so determined a voice that the pony immediately obeyed.

"I was right," said Mrs Grant.

Later that morning, Sophie, wearing a hard hat that had belonged to the Grants' daughter, rode Lucky up the long drive to Balnacraig. Mr Grant had already driven Aunt Al home because she was feeling a bit tired, and she was sitting in a chair on the lawn with Sophie's mother.

"Here comes the horsegirl," she said.

"What a nice sturdy little pony," said Sophie's mother. "Apart from the difference in colour, he reminds me of Bumblebee that Sophie rode in Cornwall."

"Lucky suits her well," said Aunt Al. "Perhaps the Grants would sell him to you."

"Oh, Aunt Al!" laughed Sophie's mother. "Wherever would we keep him? Even if we could afford him."

"Ah well," said Aunt Al. "You never know."

ABOUT THE AUTHOR

Dick King-Smith was born in 1922, and brought up in Gloucestershire. He served in the Grenadier Guards during World War II, and after the war he farmed for twenty years before becoming a full-time writer. He has three children and an army of grandchildren and great-grandchildren. He lives in a seventeenth-century cottage, three miles as the crow flies from the house where he was born.

Dick is now one of the world's favourite children's book authors. Winner of the Guardian Children's Fiction Prize for *The Sheep-Pig* (filmed as *Babe*), he was named Children's Author of the Year in 1991 and won the 1995 Children's Book Award for *Harriet's Hare*.

Dick has written over a hundred books, many of which have animal characters for the simple reason that, "I've always kept a lot of pets, I like animals, and it's fun putting words in their mouths." His farming years were the inspiration for many of his books, and pigs have featured in several of them because they are his favourite animal.